Part one

Chapter 1 – Rumination

I am a sick man. I am a spiteful man. I am an unattractive man. I believe my liver is diseased. Why is it that we admire the anti-hero more than the hero? For the same reason we don't appreciate the rich person who donates wealth, but admire the poor person who offers a pittance. It isn't the absolute, its the relative. And everything is relative.

I am a sick man, but my liver is fine as I've never been much of a drinker. The irony being that I'm filled with the bile that I spew on everyone I deem unworthy of my attention. I dabbled with psychedelics as a young man, but they didn't agree with me. I smoke the odd cigarette now and then, but that's not a habit, just to settle the nerves. The meditativeness of the deliberate inhales and exhales feel like the immortal gales blowing across the earth. I know meditation works, but I don't practice it. I don't believe in God, but when I'm in times of trouble I still find myself praying to be saved, Pascal's wager to the rescue. I consider myself a logical man, but my behaviours would disagree, and I am what I repeatedly do. I am contrarian to my core. I even contradict myself!

Speaking of what I repeatedly do, every day I walk along the tombolo to the island, which isn't really an island, but its known locally as the island. It's a very old, inactive volcano with not much of a climb to the top, like a hunched old man who no longer has the gumption for life. Its littered with tiny beaches and alcoves; plenty of places to hide away from the mundane and the eyes. There is a small fishing village to the east with a natural bay, where the local fishermen trade with the restaurants. The rest is just hillsides which is left to hikers, tourists and wildlife. Every morning, I walk with the dogs around the hiking trail, down through the beaches and finish in the village with a coffee and some feed for the dogs (the fishermen usually throw them their unsellable scraps). The trees communicate to me as I go, I see their age and their mood in the colour of the leaves. They tell me if they had a good sleep or if they were haunted by the sounds of humans and engines, roaring like a panther proclaiming his regalness from atop the apex.

The beaches are the highlight and I always go barefoot. The sand feels young; not so refined yet, with large crystalled pebbles that stick to your ocean-wet skin and drop off as you move. When the tide is out you can lap the whole island. When it's not, it conveniently ushers you toward the village. Now that I think of it, that was probably deliberate by the first settlers in the village. Clever clogs. I wonder what other things I take for granted because they were established before my time.

I've walked this route so many times I know every nook of it and there's one place I'm convinced I'm the only person to ever find. This is where I come to day-dream. My body needs physical space for my mind to find the ethereal room to wander in. I've always had an active imagination, even as a child. My brother and I would play spacemen but he never seemed to be as involved in it as I was. I could feel the change of gravity on my body and hear the echo of the spacesuit as I spoke. In fact, I found it difficult to switch back to reality once we stopped playing. I would hop and lunge around the garden like I had seen the astronauts on TV would on the moon.

This morning, as the sun rose, a beautiful dew had settled on the grass and a mist was rising as I tried to walk into it, but it was always a stone's throw ahead of me. It had a distinctive coastal smell of lightly salted, vaporised water with a hint of cut grass. The seagulls seemed to be enjoying it as much as I was, as they screeched above and swooped down at every opportunity to steal unguarded food that the locals would leave behind as they bristled about. Everyone in the town is always busy going about their own business, they offer a polite hello as they pass but nobody engages in actual conversation, which I appreciate. My own mind intrigues me more than any dullards conversation or small talk.

I get to my usual spot on the beach, perched on a splintered boulder and set down my coffee. Two large stones behind me note the burial grounds of lost souls that only I seem to come to pay tribute to, I feel it has become my burden to honour them. This is also my favourite place to draw. I take out my pen and notepad and start to sketch away, even though I'm not very good at it. I did take an art class once, but it didn't live up to my expectation of what was "artistic"; too many rules. I don't respect rules for the sake of it. And so I just wait for the universe to seed me with an idea instead. Hopefully something clever.

I wonder how many of those around me are a functional psychopath? One thing psychopaths do is over share at the beginning to make them seem vulnerable and trust worthy. It's akin to an emotional bid "I tell you something personal. Now you". Quid pro quo, Clarice. So here's something about me – I'm a direct descendant of Machiavelli himself.

The place is live is called Talam. It encompasses the whole world, or what's left of it. We have one race, called the Duine. While most Duine are of the same social class, there is a leader class called the Protos and their speakers who disseminate their laws and dictations. These speakers are called the Zealots and they usually come from the working class. Turncoats who think they can have a better life if they suckle at the teat of those above them. Cowards.. I don't trust the Protos or the

Zealots, but there isn't much I can do to affect them. So I just go about my day, like a busy bee, pollinating with my ideas, stinging the odd person who chooses to disturb me.......

The Protos, or as I like to call them, the Geek Gods (it annoys me that I thought this would be funny, but I won't erase it, out of spite to myself and to ensure absolute honesty and integrity), lied to us, but as false deities tend to do they treated it like benevolence. The megalomaniac trips to Talam's outer atmosphere and moons, the promises of sustainable energy being just around the corner, the destruction of the planet, the world-wide eradication of flora and fauna; all hidden smoke and mirror attempts to distract us from the incoming resource shortages. Talam has been hollowed out, literally and metaphorically. It took hundreds of millions of years for the fuels we use today to be created and it took us less than three hundred years to squander it all. The law of conservation of energy states that energy can neither be created nor destroyed - only converted from one form of energy to another. Despite this being known for decades, they never realised a way to close the loop on carbon to recapture, reuse and reintroduce it back to the cycle. If only they had listened to me! I had some great ideas that I could never get into the hands of the right person, who was high enough to enact them. I see the future, I see where it all goes and leads. In the future I have a daughter, a rebel! I try to communicate with her and guide her, I hope she listens to me.

We simply grew too fast, a symptom of our collective hubris. The total population never exceed one billion people for over thirteen thousand years, yet once it exceeded one billion it then hit as high as eleven billion in just three hundred years, thanks to a rapid sequence of short term technological advances that we swiftly took advantage of. A thirteen fold increase in about two percent of the time. In truth, it may be that the number that can be sustainably maintained on the planet is less than two billion, meaning we need a diaspora in the billions to the solar system and beyond, or we can wait until we kill each other off to the appropriate level in the ensuing resource wars. I firmly believe this is both plan a and b of the Protos, although they'll never confirm that. Dunbar's number be damned.

In response to this emergency a tremendous amount of time, effort and money is being spent of the dream of "visiting" other planets. The advances in virtual reality technology alongside bionic limbs and appendages facilitate spacefaring in ways once thought unimaginable. We started to augment our bodies with robotic limbs that could be controlled by the mind. Initially, an amazing leap forward for those afflicted with such tragic maladies where they lost limbs and required a bionic replacement, no more phantom pain - but I could see where it was going. Why just create an arm or a leg. Why not both, why not the torso and organs too. If all you needed was the brain, the body was no longer required. Thankfully, they didn't remove our brains and place them inside bionic bodies, like a new age Frankenstein's monster. No no. The next best thing was to create a full bionic body that we could control with our mind, without being connected to it; our doppelganger. Not quite telepathy, as it required coded receivers embedded into the cranial vault of the android and the person, to enable wireless communication. Quite genius. A complete body double to engage in the world for you. Impervious to insult and harm, indefatigable, physically superior in every way. To top it off, it was even solar powered. All while your brain and body stay in the luxury of your own home in your warm cosy bed. The world is full of danger, but if your bionic self is damaged, not to worry, send it for repair. You could also do your part for the planet and consume less, as you don't need the calories if you aren't doing the work. They were clever in rollout – it was initially used by those working on the high-risk jobs such as mining and oil rigs, but this was just to work out the kinks and effectively train and acclimatise us for what was to come. The same mineral mining on other planets. They just needed to extend the connection capacity to an interstellar bandwidth. Work from home has a new bag – you don't work an office job, you pop on your headset and sensors and pilot your android, digging mines off world. I haven't yet seen it with my own eyes but according to some it is fully functional, and they are currently working on terraforming the spaces we plan to inhabit so when the Noah's Arks arrive (by two, by two) they will be able to have a welcome party for them. Others say it is just an ambitious idea, hundreds of years away – but the proof of the pudding is in the eating, and I don't intend on eating that pudding if it can be avoided. I'll keep my feet on the ground.

This all went hand in hand with the recognition that Talam was over-populated and now, with a work force of solar powered bionic people effectively doubling the population, it was decided that world-wide, a one child per family policy would be enforced and to have this one child, you must be married, and you can't have children in more than one marriage. If you attempted to have a second child, a forced abortion would be carried out on the spot. The logic was sound, if two people can only produce one more, then each generation you half your population. After a few generations, the population has corrected itself. This, however, was met with outrage, as you could expect, but it was enforced anyway. This led to many people going off the grid or trying to at least. But most failed. They became too accustomed to the luxuries of modern life. Hot water, hot food, hot coffee. All very difficult to achieve consistently if you opt out of regular society. Then, even with these extreme measures, the leaders of the world began to recognize that the resources of Talam were being consumed at a rate far greater than we could renew them, which meant that starvation and war was on the horizon. So began a new era space race and the brainstorming of our best and brightest. Some wanted to dig for geo-thermal energy, and some wanted to use nuclear power plants, but this was too little too late. Some wanted to relocate and terraform the closest moons and planets. But one clever group decided to combine the aforementioned technological advances of VR, solar and bionics and created an army of robotic slaves that could be controlled from home, that they could send into space for exploration. The unbelievable thing was that it worked, and it was revolutionary. All leaders and investors directed all their wealth, talent, and resources behind this and for once we had a unified, global project. We quickly colonized the surrounding moons with these androids, losing many along the way (but lost souls these then became spare parts for the next generation of androids that were sent over). Nearby planets were next. The colonisation of the planets was typically tactical. The first planet targeted was due to the "fact" it rains diamonds there. Apparently, at depths of thousands of kilometres the pressure and temperature are so extreme that they can cause carbon atoms to come together and form diamond crystals. These diamonds would be brought back to Talam to make new, more durable androids. Diamonds are the hardest known natural substance, which makes them extremely useful and valuable. They are used as cutting and grinding tools in industries such as mining, construction, and machining, exactly what was needed. Diamonds also have unique electrical properties and can be used as semiconductors in high-power electronics, and they have excellent thermal conductivity, which makes them valuable for thermal management in electronic devices. We relentlessly mined all resources from the surrounding planets and created a new golden age. But we were the same evolved apes and savages as always and once the larger pie had been cooked, the powerful began to fight for how big their slice was, and they were all prepared to fight to the death for it.

Mass migration of displaced populations due to floods and famines back home were becoming common place. This resulted in a reduction in quality of life also for the populations they encroached upon. Ironically, the same people who blame the immigrants for their loss of quality of life are also the same people who wanted to be on the spaceships that left the planet to new terrains. A classic Russell conjugation; one man's asylum seeker is another's illegal immigrant. The mainland was overrun by food theft and murders. If a person has meat on their bones, it means they have food in their cupboards. The island nations, with their difficult to navigate coasts and unique environments, along with their self-sufficient structures based around natural energy such as wind and hydrothermal activity meant they have remained relatively stable. Similarly the nations outside of extreme weather zones became lush green lands and used their own inclement weather for their advantage in food production (of which, it was now illegal to export). So now we teeter on the edge of the realm of the haves and the have-nots. The haves will look after their own and ensure they have at least the bare minimum plus a reserve, just in case. The have-nots will want an equal share of everything for everyone (which is their lie, they just want for themselves and trojan horse it inside altruism), not realizing the lack of resources meant this would mean death for us all. Equality only works when everyone goes to zero.

The universe however is not without humour. As we accelerated toward our own demise, we created the perfect environment for Talam to thrive once we left - all that carbon will be devoured by the plant life as soon as vacate, the rising sea levels will create extra streams and rivers leading to better irrigation systems throughout the current dry lands. A new green age for the planet to flourish and thrive in once we the parasites have left.

For those without a future, they have the option to volunteer to take the journeys to the Solar System, believing the propaganda that they would find only wealth and abundance when they arrived on the newly terraformed areas. If it can rain diamonds, imagine the other riches on offer. However to those who knew their history, they remember that this seemed awfully similar to the tales of the "new world" and indentured servitude masquerading as opportunity to the famine generations of years gone by. Some will choose to stay, opting to believe the devil they know being better than the devil they didn't. Still, not all brave souls who make these journeys do so out of desperation. Instead, they do it out of what they believe to be their duty. It is the duty of all to seed the universe with as much life as we can to make sure we don't die here. It has been said that love is the death of duty but for many it's the reverse. Ultimately, it comes down to one's motivation to prove oneself. I always felt that I, as a competent man, could conquer any domain if given sufficient time and leverage - but the right woman can never be conquered. She can only be loved, in the hope that she loves you back.

But, for the lesser men who can't dream to be worthy of that love, or who fear not having their love returned, they satiate and abate that need of a woman for accomplishment through the misplaced and overvalued sense of "duty". If they can't love a woman, they can pretend to love a nation. They march forward into the firing line, as lost men have always done. The disposable man and rightly so; If the typical woman can give birth up to a maximum of 30 times, yet the man is capable of limitless attempts at reproduction, then this suggests on the face of it that the man is more valuable for his output can be greater. However, the reverse is true and paradoxically so. Our very existence has always depended on having as many women as possible, yet we only require a few high-quality men to seed them. Thus, results in the pattern we see across all history – the disposable man. Thrown into the belly of the beast to satiate it once more, even just for a moment. I refuse to be eaten.

Besides the only true noble duty that exists is that of the executioner, who kills the wolf to protect the sheep, only for the sheep to bah and slander him for murder. Yet still he accepts this responsibility. He lies in bed knowing the wolf was not his enemy, that the wolf was only doing as wolves do. But transgressions must be settled for and the reaper nor the hangman are ever left out of pocket.

Now, enough romance and proselytizing. Where was I. Ah, yes. The food chain of the planet is broken because of us, leaving it out of a state of equilibrium but we have left the conditions for the planet's vegetation to thrive once we leave. The excess levels of carbon in the atmosphere will mean an abundance for the flora to convert to glucose during photosynthesis. Speaking of photosynthesis, this is the holy grail of energy. The green plants are the most natural life we have as they feed off light, water, and carbon (that is, they only consume molecules, they don't require death to feed). Simple, efficient, stable. Fast forward to the herbivores, the first cheaters in the process. Why perform photosynthesis when you can just eat the things that do. Clever, but the universe giveth and it taketh away. The carnivores added a further layer of complexity to this process, further removing themselves from heliotropic equilibrium. Then, Consciousness. Consciousness has no purpose in the heliotropic world. It is a vestigial solution to the problems created by complexity in the food chain. It is a product of competition, intelligent life should move away from it due the to harm it causes. So, at least in my estimation, the process of evolution isn't a process of progress but one of deleteriation. An energy arms race to the bottom. The conscious being can only consume through destruction and then flog itself. Masochism at its finest. It is why we maintain a death instinct despite our "intelligence". We long to be returned to the soil and to escape our consciousness. We only find peace when reabsorbed into the planet. Maybe is this why reincarnation became a concept. You go as many times as you need to be a good person. I often find myself thinking about this when the sun hits my face, and about the fusion process that is taking place on its surface. If aliens did visit us, why would they be interested in us? Surely, they would learn more about survival from the organisms who eat the waste product of a burning star, rather than from those who burn the sludge of creatures who died millions of years ago to power our vehicles. We haven't even figured out how to use the rain cycle to produce clean drinking water, or an efficient way to desalinate ocean water. Philistines.

One of the reasons why photosynthesis is so efficient is because it takes advantage of the quantum mechanical properties of light, which allows it to absorb photons of light with very high efficiency. In addition, the pigments in plants and algae that are responsible for capturing light energy, such as chlorophyll, are highly specialized to absorb light in the wavelengths that are most abundant in sunlight; god bless evolution. Our best scientists have been trying to mimic this, working on the idea of using a sun trap or a mini Dyson-sphere, to trap solar energy to feed the consumerism we require. Maybe then we can return to a vegetative state and absorb sunlight for fuel as the plants do.

Not everyone is as reserved as I, though. The first off-world voyages have begun preparation with the selection process dividing into two camps. The educated class and the working class. They aren't calling it that, but it's clear to see the difference between the processes. If you're an engineer, doctor, food scientist, botanist – you're first class. If you're a factory worker who has dreams of striking it rich, you can queue at the back with the rest of the plebeians. Give your children to Ceaser and he'll give you back good Romans. I know time travel isn't real because the first thing I would do is visit myself at this moment. Or this one. Or maybe it is real, and my life turns out exactly how I want it to and so I have no need to revisit myself to make adjustments. This latter idea warms my cockles and invigors me to doubly redouble strokes upon my foe entropy. More strokes than you could shake-a-spear at.

Anyway, I have trust issues. I know my own senses lie to me, so why would I trust anything else. If you give me no reason to distrust you, isn't that exactly what an untrustworthy person who planned to betray me would do? I see your game. That's why I feel most comfortable in those who live with warts and all. I observe patterns over time and build predictability models for each person. If you subvert these patterns, you either have now shown your true colours and were lying all along, or you have grown. Show me the evidence of your growth or I will take it as evidence of your betrayal. My walls are high, they are guarded and barbed. Exit is easy, but entry takes a lifetime, or a life. Speaking of senses, if I had your eyes transplanted into my sockets, would I see colours differently? Almost certainly yes, your cones are not my cones and your rods not mine. So how can we agree on colours? Yes, there is the subjective colour, I'm aware. The length of the wave that corresponds with each colour. But our subjective experience of colour is entirely different and in an inconsequential way. Is our reality just a shared, unspoken agreement that as long as our subjective experiences are relatively similar enough, we can just ignore the differences? If so, then Zarathustra was right when he spoke thusly; you have your way, I have my way, as for the right way, the correct way, and the only way, it does not exist. But I find this unfulfilling. If philosophy is just applied psychology, which is applied biology, which is applied chemistry, which is applied physics, which is just applied math – the universe is then just an unknowable (due to the limitations of our intelligence) but known (due to our awareness of our limitations) quantity; then the only way does exist, and Nietzsche (or more accurately, Zarathustra) was wrong. For their can only be one way and it is mathematically provable. That one way is the moment the entire universe is in existence in each moment and has been since the Big Bang occurred and every quark and gluon has acted predictably as they do ever since. Our only limitation is that we lack the understanding. In that sense, time doesn't exist, it is merely a changing of states of being for the universe in a calculable direction. If you were able to move every iota of the universe back to the place it was five seconds ago, you would have technically reversed time back to that moment. Ah, we've returned to time travel, which is ironic. Let us move forward instead, through time, at the appropriate rate of one second per second. Firstly though, I'd like to expand on the universe, as if it doesn't expand enough on itself. I am obsessed with the fractal. I see no difference between the nervous system, the roots of a plant, the branches of a tree, the axons and dendrites of a cell, the road systems (seen from a map), the flow of water and electricity. They reach for connections and vie for the path of least resistance. Another example of fractal is the bacteria in your gut. It doesn't realize it is just bacteria performing a duty within a biome but aren't we the same. Inconsequential individuals performing a minor duty as part of the collective, a simple node in a complex network. Is the universe just the gut of a celestial being? Did the universe create us to learn how to reverse entropy, to prevent its own heat death, the same way we rely on our gut biome to digest our food? These are just the thoughts of a lucid dreamer maybe. Maybe we are just the dreams and thoughts of a greater creature, given how superfluous and grandiose the setting and how dilated the time is in a dream while you are in it, it isn't inconceivable to me. How much time has really passed? Even if time is just a construct. I'll say instead, in which moment in the universe, where all of its contents are assimilated in a given way, are we currently in?

I've done it again. Digressions will be the death of me. My pipe is almost empty, so I better stop faffing about and judging. The sun sets soon, and I am a useless idiot after dark. The early bird may catch the worm, but it also lacks stamina for the night.

Besides, my beloved awaits, and she doesn't like to sleep alone.

Chapter 2 – School

The next morning as the sun rises, it's my turn to bring the kinder to education. It is custom that each week a parent will participate in the days teachings to support the teacher and to bestow any wisdom, skills, or lessons they may have, so it is clear why they wanted me. We arrive a few moments early and are greeted by the exiting parents and the teacher, who acknowledges our arrival and so initiates the day.

"Class begins in a few moments children, please find a place to be seated." The teacher bellows authoritatively.

The children are well versed in this game of subjectiveness; there are no seats in the room. Instead, one must find a comfortable location to be seated. Another deliberancy of this request is the choice of how "time" is described. A "few moments" is entirely subjective, as "few" is not a defined quantity, nor is a "moment'. So why this peculiarity? Since moving away from traditional timekeeping and back to a heliocentric schedule (school starts one hour after sunrise and ends at high noon). I say "time-keeping" and not "time", for time is a measure of entropy and can be treated as a universal measure when taken as the atomic second - unless of course the atomic second also changes in different places of the universe, or in different universes, probably as a result of different gravitational forces, in which case a decision must be made to either extend the agreed upon length of a second or to choose a new basis for which we hinge our concept of time upon. That is to say, for example, 9am is relative to the place you are telling the time, but one hour after sunrise is a universal all year round, assuming the distances being travelled are do-able on foot, nobody should be crossing meridian lines for an education.

My issue with our construct of time is the nature of its creation, always reverse engineering to find a suitable approach. The 24-hour clock is based on the proverbial sundial completing a 180' semi-circle (twice, one for day, 12 hours, and one for night, 12 hours, 360'). To which we turned into a clock, to represent the sun dial shadow and that each degree of the 360 is made up 60 minutes of arc and 60 minutes of arc is made up of 60 seconds. That is to say, 4 minutes of time is equal to 1 degree of movement around the 360 arc. Thus, we have the humble watch. However, I propose this was an error. Why doesn't the watch face have a top and bottom hemisphere, notated 1-12 on each, representing the day and the night. At least this would then be grounded in the foundational notion that we are tracking the sun, to represent a day, as opposed to the abstractness of how we currently tell time.

However, that does create another issue which has been at the centre of my thoughts on quite many topics lately; does time matter in an environment that does not have sunrise or sunset? What will we, and by we, I mean those leaving the planet as our representatives, as I myself have no intention to ever leave, synchronise our clocks to. Will we evolve away from being essentially sun driven, diurnal, circadian creatures? …. I'm stuck in my own head again and class is about to start.

"So, children who can described what a chair is?"

Arms extend skyward as if their hands are trying to leap from their body. Excited children, eager to impress, as good studiousness is rewarded and cherished. Although I notice my own not participating, I'll need to ask them why, later.

"It has four legs!" a child shouts.

"Ah, yes, but so does a cat, is a cat a chair? Is a chair a cat?" I reply, to the sniggers of a few children who are tickled by the thought of using a cat to sit on.

"It's made of wood and comes with kitchen table!"

"You are not wrong, but you are not correct. A chair is something that we use for sitting on, when we need somewhere to sit, and both criterions are critical. Which means, an object isn't defined by its objective features. No, its defined by its subjective qualities and functions, by how it used. There is no reality for a chair, only what we perceive the chairs reality to be based upon its usefulness to us in any given instance. Therefore, reality itself doesn't exist. Only perception and projection of each respective reality exists. If there is nothing perceived or to be perceived, does reality stop existing? Does anybody know what that means?"

The awkward silence was permitted to hang in the room for a moment, although most of the children have no idea, there is at least one who thinks they know but are too afraid to answer, for fear of being mocked for being wrong, or being mocked for being correct.

"Let me ask it a different way - if a tree falls in the woods and nobody is around to hear it, did it make a sound?"

I write it on the board for all to see and then asks them to copy it down, word for word, onto the very back page of their notebooks.

"My promise to each of you is that by the time we reach that note on the last page of your book, you will understand and what's more, you will be able to answer it."

The teacher takes over with their last command of the day; *"For tomorrow's lesson, I want you all to read the poem titled Wendigo and we'll discuss."*

Wendigo. Vacuous and haunched by the body. Body of water, to be replenished. I drink but am never quenched. I feast but am always famished. I eat myself by eating my own, but my soul is hardly nourished. The moon covers its eyes with rolling clouds. It doesn't want to be seen. It doesn't want to see the spilled blood of the lamb. Spindling limbs move through the lake, washing the blemished spirit than can never be clean. Once a devil, never sainted. Capillary waves rippling away remind of the choices that can't be undone and consequences that can only be accepted, tainted forever. Sun will rise soon but the light will only keep me at bay, for I do not exist in time, and I have no regrets. I'm a shadow. One that no light will fall on. If you follow me, you'll never see the day. I devour energy and return nothing. I cannot lose because I've already lost it all.

On the walk home, I recall the discreetness of the children in the class and ask them why they didn't have their hands up when I asked the questions.

"Because you always say, "only donkeys and mules make shows of courage". We both knew the answer but didn't need advertise it to get kudos"."

I've never been prouder.

"I didn't think you were listening to me."

"We weren't, you just say it so often that it kinda stuck."

On the way home we stop off in the market for vegetables and meats for dinner, I'm planning a stew tonight. I love a good stew; my poor grandmother was always a terrible cook but she could make a great stew that would feed us for days. It is the perfect meal for after a long day to refuel the body, or as comfort food to nourish the soul. I enter the butchers (who's also the greengrocer thankfully) to pick up the items needed for dinner.

"Howya Bill?"

"Not too bad, and yourself?"

"Ah yeah, keeping busy. Did you get my order off Eve this morning?"

"I did indeed, I have it here ready and waiting for ya. She paid for it too, so you're all boxed off."

"Fantastic."

She's a divil for that, but there's no stopping her. I can only begrudgingly acquiesce, but in truth I do love it about her. We move on from the market and just before we arrive home, we bump into a classmate's parent. An odiousness repugnance of a man who winks at everyone. His winks to women are always sexually suggestive. His winks at men are condescending and unctuous. I hate when people wink at me - it deprives me of my ability to disagree. How do I disagree with a wink! It's as if an anchor is thrown into your flesh that can't be extracted. I dodge his impedimenting conversation with an obviously false excuse (deliberately obvious so he gets the hint) and we continue our way. We get home before Eve, so I make a start on dinner and the kids help, eagerly setting the table (they get extended play time based on the amount of chores they help with. Never underestimate the right incentive structure). Eve arrives home just in time, and we devour the food. Once the kids finish, I send them upstairs to wash up while Eve and I get to cleaning up.

"Do you miss your gran?

"Of course I do, why do you ask?"

"I mean today, specifically. You usually make stew when you're thinking of her."

"Oh, I didn't realize I did that, but now that you mention it, her birthday is coming up and I've been thinking about visiting the grave soon."

"You should bring the kids this time. They need to learn about death at some stage."

"I know, you're right. I'm just eager to preserve their innocence as much as possible. We can't unscramble that egg."

"Who said it needs to be unscrambled?"

"Fine fine fine. Leave it with me. Do you want to join for the bedtime story?"

"No no, I need some alone time to process the day and unwind. I'll go sit in the garden, it's a clear night and dark enough now I should be able to see the stars. Come down to me when you're done."

"I will of course my love."

The boys hear the creaking of the stairs as I walk up and use this as their opportunity jump into bed and pretend to be asleep. Clever boys, but they don't yet realise I was also once a clever boy and clever boys grow into clever men. Still though, I let them think it worked.

Chapter 3 – Job Advertisement

Today is a day for myself so after a few hours splitting wood and harvesting, I pop into town to knit some stratagems together. First stop, the butchers again.

"Have you seen the new job ads Mephi?"

My mother named me Mephi as, according to her when I was born, I crowned as the sunrise was coming through the hospital window and she thought of Mephistopheles, the devil in Faust, and how it was linked to Lucifer, the morning star.

"Why would a retired man be looking at jobs ads?"

"You're not old enough to be retired!"

"No, but I am wealthy enough. Now, what's it about the ads that has your interest piqued?"

"Let me read it to you."

"A state-backed intergalactic team is being created to be comprised of all backgrounds and skillsets – if you are interested in being at the forefront of new frontiers and have any of the following skillsets or similar, please contact your local office. Details of the nationwide offices can be found overleaf."

"Wow, so it is true. What are the skillsets they're looking for?"

"Oh, interested all of a sudden, are we? Sure, you wouldn't be able to leave that wife of yours alone for a week, never mind eighteen months!"

"I'd rather lose sight of the sun and never feel its warmth on my skin again than leave her for eighteen months."

"Ah shtop, you sappy idiot. Anyway, why are you asking about skillsets? Are you interested?"

"Absolutely not, just trying to glean what they're up to exactly."

"Well, glean away. They want all kinds of farmers, botanists, tradesmen and carpenters, engineers and so on. Pretty much everything. Seems like they really do want to build a new world up there. They're even re-deploying parts of the fonctionnaire to recruit for it!".

The fonctionnaire are a special branch of the civil service. Kafkaesque in how they operate but only used on matters of the utmost importance. They should try and fix this world first. Feels like we're just giving up on it and running away. Maybe there's something they aren't telling us, an incoming, incipient natural disaster that can't be avoided. Still though, I think I'll stay here all the same thank you very much. And why are they being so open with the recruitment, I told them, the mid-level employees are the key to success. The lowest don't want help, the highest don't need help, the middle need it but don't know how to ask. But this looks like they just wanted to hoover up the lowest, maybe it's lambs to slaughter, pawns to sacrifice, until they get a better handle on things."

"Anyway, got any fresh liver? And some bones for the dogs too if you could please."

"No liver I'm afraid, we had a small amount this week. I'll save you some Monday when we get the next batch in."

"Feck, cheers. Just the bread so."

"Bread it is, and I'd suggest buying these bones here and use the marrow on the bread. Delicious. Then throw the bones and leftovers to the dogs."

"Perfect, thanks again."

Good food leads to a good soul. Not that I believe in souls, but more so the spirit of the thing (no pun intended). I better dig around to see if I can find out anything further on this new job ad. It's getting too close to home, and I didn't expect it so soon. I wonder what stage they're at, if they've perfected Dyson-spheres like in the sketches I sent to them, or if they're still testing soils for minerals. The bastards are rushing it. What are they not telling us! Anyway, enough of the misplaced anger. Those who over-indulge in their emotions are committing a form of masochistic masturbation. It's more pleasureful to lean into it, commit a crime and blame the emotions than to soothe the ache and use reason. A crime of passion? Bah! A crime of self-indulgence.

After milling around for a bit and not getting much more information, I head home to chat to Eve. She won't be pleased to hear about the new job ads. Especially given she has family who are looking for work and are likely to be targeted by the government recruiters. When I arrive home, her sister is already there, and I can hear them talking about it.

"It's like the gold rush out West, they are promising our good young men they can be space cowboys mining for riches and controlling androids better than their video games. I don't like this, it's brainwashing!"

Feck, I'm too late. Eve will be wound up later. I push through the door, pretending I don't know what the mood is.

"Hiya love, no liver but I did get bread and marrow. The kids washed?"

"Yes yes, they're upstairs waiting for your story time."

I place the shopping in the kitchen and make my way upstairs. As I walk up, I notice all the smudges on the walls and ceiling from all of the different bugs I've squished over the years. My walls are an insect cemetery. I need to paint them soon. The kids heard me coming and jump into bed, pretending they weren't doing something they weren't supposed to.

"Well! If it isn't my favourite troublesome twosome. What's the plan for tonight."

"NEW STORY!"

"New story it is!"

I settle into my seat and get comfortable.

"I used to live in an old village. In this village there was an old king, who loved being King and loved his lands and his people and the people loved him. He had been King for a long time and began to think about when he might die and what will happen after he's gone. He grew fearful of this as time progressed, so sought the wisdom of the old sage. The sage shared with the king a powerful drink filled with herbs and plants which were designed to help the drinker to open their mind to the universe, and the sage urged the King that the only way to continue living is to seek death. The old King didn't really understand this advice as it didn't make sense to him. He went back to his normal ways and then one night, in a dream, death came for him. The king bargained with death until a deal was struck. Death's champion was looking for a challenge, as no mortal man was able to match his might so far. The

deal was this – every day, the King would send one champion of his own to the top of the mountain to fight Death's champion. If the King's champion ever won, the king would then be granted immortality. If the king's champion didn't win, then he could always try again the next day, as the king would be guaranteed another 24 hours of life at least, as long as he sent a new challenger. The king grew excited. The thoughts of immorality plagued his mind. He could conquer death after all!

And so, it began. Day after day, the King sent champion after champion, the best of the best, to death. For the King considered it his duty to remain King so he could continue to rule in prosperity for the good of the people, that was his right and duty as King. Some wanted to go, as they knew the bounty they would receive for victory from the King would mean they would never want again. Most though were terrified, for they knew that the best men were sent first and had already gone and lost, that they had little hope to survive. Husbands, fathers, brothers, sons, uncles. All slain for the whim of a mad man. Families destroyed. Thousands of fighters needlessly perished. Death congratulated himself for concocting such a masterful agreement, as no man has ever defeated death.

Instead, the kingdom lost all its best men and as a result, fell into ruin. With no men around the woman began to leave also. The old King, now significantly older, realised the error of his ways. He should not have tried to run from death, but instead embrace it, like the sage advised, to use his remaining time to serve his people, to be a good King and to be memorialised in their traditions. To have great stories told about his nobleness and to live on in their memories. Instead, his Kingdom destroyed, his lineage and heirs fallen to death's champion and thrown as ashes to the wind. On his last day of life, death revisited and asked the old King if, before he died, he wished to see the face of the champion who had slain his greatest warriors and destroyed his

Kingdom. The King nodded in agreement and took one last look up as the hooded figure removed his disguise to reveal the face of the Sage. The King wept a pitiful cry and filled with remorse and regret, asked for Death to finally take him.

The King had realised upon seeing him again, Death had set him up. He sent the Sage, who could see the Kings innermost fears and that his intentions would lead to the sinister actions that followed. Once the King announced the intentions to send fighters to the Champion, the Sage struck his own deal with Death. The Sage would become a new Champion of death in exchange for saving the lives of the warriors the King had sent to be slaughtered. These men instead would be offered new homes and shelters away from the kingdom and they could start anew, without a tyrant King to rule over them. As time passed by, they were also able to smuggle the women from the kingdom into the new townships and they could set up new lives."

"So, can anyone tell me the moral of the story? No?"

"If you let your fears guide you, you will lose everything you love, and it'll be by your own hand that you lost it. Be a good king for your people – they deserve it and so do you. Tomorrow night, I'll tell you the second part of the story! Now, goodnight little ones."

They hate a cliff-hanger but that's my favourite part. It gives me something to look forward to, to get me through the day tomorrow. I trot back downstairs and thankfully the visitor has left. Not that I don't like company, just not at the end of a long day.

I can see Eve is ready for war, so I brace myself as I enter.

"I swear, she never sees bad news coming until it smacks here in the face. Ever the optimist that one."

"If you're wearing rose tinted glasses, you can't see the flags that are red too. What's it this time?"

"She's afraid her boy will apply for these nonsense jobs. They're calling them space cowboys now, great marketing. How can we compete with that to keep them here? What do we have to offer, farms or forestry or digging peat?"

"I know, I know. We can't compete, we just have to hope they can get through this period and age out of that need for adventure. But we can't make them stay, morally or righteously, we must let them choose."

"Just once I wish you'd tell me what makes me feel better instead of a harsh truth."

"If I did you wouldn't respect me anymore."

We laugh and the mood settles. I fetch my axe from this morning and find the whetstone to sharpen it. I find the smooth and repetitive motion very soothing.

"Why do you always sharpen your axe when you sit down by the fire?"

"So, when I need it I don't have to sharpen it."

Chapter 4 - Recruiters

A small army of recruiters entered town the next morning, shouting their slogan *"The future is Venus, Mars, or in the stars"*. Catchy, I'll admit. They quickly gain the moniker of "The Redmen" from the locals due to the connection to Mars. I do wonder is it as honest as they make it out. I have no doubt that the motivation of riches could pull a man to Mars, but I can't shake the feeling that this isn't just the pull factor of wealth. What are the push factors? Is there something around the corner for us that is going to end our time here? I mean, everything comes to an end, even the universe will eventually reach its own death, I remember that from the textbooks "the universe will evolve to a state of no thermodynamic free energy, and will therefore be unable to sustain processes that increase entropy". In other words all sources of energy move to places of no energy and right now, our energy and people are going abroad. Total stable equilibrium. Then bang. A big one. A new universe begins. Or so I believe. That was how our Big Bang occurred. We aren't the first or only Universe. Death and rebirth. Complete entropy, all energy turned to heat and dissipated across infinity. Then what? Size is relative and time is warped by gravity. We're told that prior to the Big Bang, the entire universe was condensed into a miniscule area and then exploded outward and has continued to expand outward ever since, at an accelerating rate. But it is my conjecture that this was itself a full universe prior to ours, that we can only perceive as being small, in the same way the next universe will perceive us after our own heat death and resulting big bang. So in a way, the universe is a living being, that dies and gives birth to an heir. So, on that basis, are we just it's thoughts and dreams? Maybe the universe created us deliberately, so we can figure out a way to avoid it's death and save it. Would this be god? Wouldn't that be ironic that God didn't create man as an act of benevolent creation but instead as a hail Mary (pardon the pun) to save itself?

Speaking of God, I always despised the idea of Religion. Opiate of the masses and so on. Sit, stand, kneel, obey. A pious man behaves with decency out of fear and reverence of a deity. No more than a coward looking after his own interests. A man that behaves with decency in spite of knowing that God doesn't exist, that's true nobility. I always wondered why the Devil was seen as being in opposition to God. That is, when you break a commandment, you are damned to Hell and punished by Satan. He wants to bring us light and feed us the fruit of knowledge. The serpent who improved our vision. It seems to me like Satan is God's executioner. Here we are again, back to noble executioners. Furthermore, the other names associated are Lucifer aka the Lightbringer and the Morning Star (coincidentally names associated with the Planet Venus, for how bright it appears in our night sky). The Greco-Romans considered Venus to be the child of Aurora - Aurora meaning "light" the Latin name Dawn. The Light's Son, the Dawn. The morning sun. The irony of this is not lost on me. The Romans deified Venus and she encompassed love, beauty, desire, sex, fertility, prosperity, and victory.

"How you have fallen from heaven, morning star! You have been cast down you who once laid low the nations! You said in your heart, "I will ascend to the heavens; I will raise my throne above the stars of God; I will sit enthroned on the mount of assembly, on the utmost heights of Mount Zaphon. I will ascend above the tops of the clouds; I will make myself like the Most High." But you are brought down to the realm of the dead, to the depths of the pit. Those who see you stare at you, they ponder your fate: "Is this the man who made kingdoms tremble, the man who made the world a wilderness, who overthrew its cities and would not let his captives go home?" Pride and ambition will be the downfall of good men…. Maybe. But this seems to me like the perfect way to ensure nobody will try to rise above God, to deliberately have your ally attempt to do so only to fall, as a lesson to everyone else for what will happen if they try. An inside job if you will. Satan is the sun trying to keep us alive, God is the universe trying to consume us. It seems to me that Satan is the real hero of this story, deliberately playing bad cop and taking the fall so the children will eat their vegetables and obey. I appreciate bad cops and executioners. They perform the duties the weak-willed pretend don't exist. Hawks and Doves. The

world needs a few Hawks so the Doves can spread love. I'm happy to be a Hawk. Or at least I convince myself I am, to cover my lack of love to spread.

Anyway, on with the day. I chat with a few different recruiters to see what message they're trying to spread. They all pretty much said the same thing, which means they've been trained and drilled well. This isn't being left to the amateurs that's for sure. The last one I spoke to said "Wouldn't it be great if we could just time travel and be there already". I acquiescently laughed in agreement, without wanting to open up a dialogue with him about time travel, he didn't seem to be intelligent enough. Also because I already know time travel back-wards isn't real. I have a safe word, so that if I ever do discover time travel, I'll know it's me (and not an imposter trying to trick me). That hasn't happened yet, ergo, it doesn't happen in my lifetime. Besides, to travel back in time, you would have to move every single quark in the universe and reverse it back to where it was in the moment you would like to travel to (am I repeating myself again?)... Anyway, in other words, you would require infinite knowledge of the universe and infinite energy to do so. Or maybe you could isolate a local section of space time and just do it there. Which isn't totally preposterous I suppose. Given that time slows down around highly dense objects due to their gravity, that means every local spot has their own time (local being relative of course). Although, if you were to reverse the quarks of the universe, you would also have to do so on yourself, which would effectively reverse your memory (as your memory is a function of the structure of your brain, which would also be rewinding, so to speak) of it and so you would reverse time and then not remember that you did it. Unless you were able to step into your own local time universe, reverse the time of the overall universe and then step back out. Then, possibly, you would remember.

Additionally, to travel forward in time at a rate faster than your local rate, you would need to either leave that local rate of time or create a sub-local time that exerts it effects only on you. Then while, say, one day passes in your time, you arrive in the local time five days later. Everyone else experience time as normal and are now five days older but you experience time relative to yourself. So, in essence, you haven't travelled forward in time, you have just slowed your own relative time, or just stood next to an extremely dense object with an unfathomable gravitation pull, without being crushed into spaghetti. So, both time travel forward and backward are do-able, just not by you or I, or anyway in existence that we know of. Similarly, if time slows down around large gravitational bodies such as a black hole, it means the universe exists across multiple timespans. The future is already here, it just isn't evenly distributed. Which creates the thought, does it have one over-arching time? Is this the time that our universal being experiences? If we do find a way to avoid the heat death of the universe, by recycling the energy effectively, doesn't that mean we will just repeat time over and over without remembering each iteration? Maybe we are already in that loop and haven't figured it out yet. I think I'd prefer death.

Now, speaking of time, it's time to head home and finish my story. I start to walk but I don't make much progress before I'm stopped by Davey, the village idiot and drunkard.

"I'm going to Mars, Mephi?"

"Are ya now? I'm surprised they'd take you."

"Very funny and yes, I signed up today. They give a signing fee and all, I'll have it in two days!"

"Ah, now it makes sense".

"Anyway, I was just wondering, would you have a lend? Just til Friday til the signing fee comes through?"

"The truth reveals itself".

"What?"

"No, I don't have a lend, I won't fund your slow descent into suicide".

"What?"

"Never mind!"

I storm off before he can ask me any other questions. I hate to lend anyone money and to be honest, I don't have it at the moment. I couldn't admit that to him, so I pretended to be outraged at the request.

I get home and just as planned, the boys are ready and waiting for their story.

"Where did we finish?"

"The old King died, and the new village was happier than ever."

"Ok, good. Let me just talk with your mother first and then I'll be up in ten."

I go into the garden and Eve gives me news on the chickens. We have three hens: Polly, Molly and Dolly. We rescued them as baby chicks a couple of years ago and raised them since and in return, they've provided us with eggs. But lately, the matriarch of the group, Molly, has been showing her age and is not laying as many eggs as she used to. Eve knows this means she'll be on the dinner table soon, c'est la vie, but she can't bring herself to think about it. I attempt to ease her mind by mentioning it means we have space to rescue more chicks, and this helps slightly. I don't envy her maternal softness, I appreciate and love it about her, but I'm also glad it isn't a burden I have to carry. The only thing I carry is my axe and I swing it wherever necessary. Next, it'll be at poor Molly's neck. But she'll nourish the family as she's always done. Her head and feet to the dogs, a Sunday roast dinner for the family and afterwards I'll make bone broth and use the left-over fat for cooking. Then whatever is left is back onto the compost pile. Every part used and Molly's essence shared amongst the place she called home. I wonder, if I died, would the animals eventually eat me? I wouldn't mind if they did, truthfully. I'd rather they use my carcass than die of starvation. One last act of usefulness. Alas, my usefulness isn't exhausted yet, but the children are, and they require a bedtime story immediately.

"So, boys. The old King has died, and the new village was firmly established and thriving. They had taken all the good things that worked in the previous village and learned new ways to prosper. They traded amongst themselves and began to specialise in certain things like crop growing, bread making, tool creating and weatherproofing garments. These advances gave them an advantage against the surrounding environment and the other distant-but-not-distant-enough village tribes. As the village grew, the elders recognised that their population would soon surpass the output the village lands could sustain and so they concluded that they had two choices; choice one was to build outward and domesticate more of the surrounding lands, choice two was invade a nearby village and take their resources. Ultimately, in time, they decided to do both, but they didn't stop at just one nearby village. They began a conquest of all that surrounded them, all that they could reach.

After some warfaring, the original elder recognised the hypocrisy of asking the men of this village to fight wars on foreign soil, after saving them from the previous king who did similar. So instead, he recommended domestication of the local lands at a mass scale and offered the other villages the opportunity to peacefully join them.

To coordinate this, they elected one who would hold ultimate decision making to guide them. Not a king, they would insist, but a leader. Originally, the people wanted the elder to be this leader, but he abstained from the nomination due to his age and the perception that he was instigating this idea just for his benefit. Instead, he argued, he would rather be counsel to the leader. A person of influence without decision making responsibility, so that when it inevitably went wrong it wouldn't be his head on the block, he jested.

So the first leader was selected, given the title of the month of his birth; July. July was a good, just leader. He wanted the best for all and didn't live a life of luxury himself. He lived with his people, ate with them and enjoyed no special privilege. In turn, the people respected him and everyone pulled their weight. He listened to the sage advice of the elder and decided to take twelve squires into his employ. These squires would be named for each of the months of the year, to signify their new ranks and life in service to the people, the one due to be named July was allowed to keep his name, Brutus, due to the clash of names (and also rumoured nepotism). They were selected for competencies they displayed in their youth, specifically those that would be beneficial to the realm. Athleticism, tactical thinking and strategy, communication, charisma and so on. This chosen dozen became known as the children of July. One child in particular stood out the as the clear apex of the twelve: Brutus. Each of the children had their own mark of brilliance and Brutus was the equal of each of them, if not better. Brutus quickly rose to be the de-facto leader of the children and was given personal tutelage by July and by the elder, until the elder passed away of old age. At the elder's funeral, Brutus was stationed at the front alongside July while the remaining children were in the common crowd. This sewed discontent into the sons who grew to hate that Brutus was better than they were and that everyone else knew it and could see it. Mutiny was a more palatable outcome than subjugation for the children. They set in motion a scheme that would result in the death of July, who was led to believe it was Brutus' betrayal that caused his demise. This broke his heart. Not only was Brutus unaware of this scheme he wasn't even in the village at the time. They deliberately waited until it was his turn to go scouting outside of the village; the children would divide into groups of four and take turns to scout lands around the village to hone their skills in hunting and prospecting. On the same night that July was murdered, the three children along with Brutus on the scouting mission waited for him to sleep before plunging their blades into his back. Leader and successor, now dead at midnight. The village ideals castrated after just one generation. The remaining sons then nominated their own leader, or more accurately, he stepped out of the shadows to emerge as their leader. You only see the predator when he wants to be seen.

Maliciously they named him August, as he followed July. They no longer wished to be called the Children, either. They now wanted to be called the Guerrillas. They decided also to bestow a name onto the village that recognised what they considered it to be – the apex, the pinnacle, the Zenith. The people will become known as Zenitians.

Their first port of call now that they had cleared the path to power, was to take control of the narrative surrounding this coup d'état. They concocted the story that July and Brutus were murdered by a chieftain of a nearby village who planned to invade now that the leadership was destroyed, and their leadership was disbanded and in disarray. They argued the best course of action was to attack that village first

33

while it was unexpected for them to do so, which would also signal their strength and unity in adversity. This was mostly met with disgust, as the villagers wanted to mourn their beloved dead. They also suspected the true nature of the murders but were too afraid to sound their dissent, given the new leaders were clearly willing to kill those in their way. The people acquiesced and permitted the pre-emptive attack on their neighbours.

At the behest of August and lead by the Guerrillas, they began the conquest of greed and glory that was masqueraded as vengeance for a loved, fallen leader. They first entered the accused village and demanded the leaders be brought out and made accountable for their actions. Those good, innocent leaders saw that if they sacrificed themselves, it would prevent a full-scale war for their people and so they surrendered themselves, hoping that they would see mercy. Instead, they were all slaughtered one by one in a public execution, a display of dominance. Immediately after the slaughter, the Guerrillas lead their fighters into the village and proclaimed it was now a land of August; to be called New Zenitia forthwith. They killed all of the men who were capable of fighting and then lay with their women, impregnating them. The women were clever and knew they would need to assimilate to survive but, they remembered all that had occurred that day. They remembered their native tongue, their stories and their loved ones who were maliciously slain. They passed these stories on to their children, born of the Guerrillas but not considered true Zenitians, instead they were called Plebes, second class citizens with second class rights. The Plebes, once grown, were used as cannon fodder in the voyages of the Guerrillas to conquer all villages and fertile lands, near and far. With more conquest came greater armies of disposable men, for men are always disposable. The village grew into an empire and August it's autocratic, dictatorial, malevolent, and omnipresent demi-deity. His power came from subjugation, performatively devouring any subordinates with the temerity to rise against him. In time, a tentative peace descended over the empire as everyone knew it wasn't worthwhile trying to gain freedom. This displeased August as he was unable to show his might, so he began to deliberately instigate uprisings through his secret police and using professional provocateurs, only to quash any uprising mercilessly and violently and publicly execute any unfortunate Plebe who dared to sympathise or join. This was the lifeblood of the reign of August, resulting in the colloquial epithet of the Plebes that August was "an immortal beast who feasts on the flesh and soul of man. The Wendigo. He'll only die when there's no one left to defy him, for there'll be no one left for him to eat.

History doesn't repeat itself, but it rhymes, and the eventual demise of August was very similar to his rise to power. After years in power and with control over the information taught in schools and disseminated in the villages, most people came to believe that August was a benevolent and good leader. Or at least, they were clever enough to know they were supposed to act that way. As part of this, August also had the idea to gather the best and brightest young children into a talent school so they could best service the empire "Give your children to August and he'll give you back good Zenitians" and through this he was able to surround himself with a clutch of brilliantly gifted men and women who were loyal to him and believed what he wanted them to believe. His favourite student was a viciously sharp, precocious girl, Medb. All great women are named Medb. She would become his personal guard, for there was nobody as skilled in combat as her, and one of his top advisors, for she was as clever as she was fierce. Furthermore, and though this was typically handled by the lower ranked judiciary members, she insisted on being the executioner-in-chief, to swing the blade herself on those that transgressed against her beloved emperor. For she insisted the job of the executioner was the most noble act a person could perform!"

The boys, flabbergasted by this statement shout in unison; *"How can it be noble to kill people!"*

"Well, if a person must die for the sins they've committed, but it is also a sin to commit murder, isn't it noble for a person to sacrifice themself and accept the sin onto themselves so that others don't have to sin? It is also a very difficult thing to take a life, not everyone has the fortitude to do so. So, it behoves those who do have the fortitude of doing difficult work to do it, no matter what. Right?"

"Remember boys, you never break the rules. Until you've mastered them, then it's your duty to break them. Rules are created to keep the unworthy from hurting themselves. If you can prove yourself by mastering the rules, they no longer apply to you. Do you understand what I'm saying?"

They both nod, but I can tell they are stunned by this and don't fully grasp it. *"Don't tell your mother I said that."*

"Medb was a loyal servant to August. Right up until she wasn't. She believed that everything August had done was for the betterment of the realm, but over time she was realising the inconsistencies, contradictions, and hypocrisies in his rule. She eventually realised he was the evil ruler subjugating his people for his own gain. For this, she waited until they were alone together and plunged her sword into his chest, killing him. This broke her heart to do so, but she knew it was the right thing to do. Just as the noble executioner should. She presented his body to the court of people gathered in the markets and declared herself a traitor, expecting to be sentenced to

death. Instead, the people rejoiced that the reign of August had come to an end and in his stead, they proclaimed Medb as their new queen."

"Now - I think that's a good place to end for tonight. Can I trust you two to head to sleep in a reasonable time if I leave you be?"

I look up and they're both fast asleep. Nothing sleeps as peacefully as a child that is loved by its mother. I sit with them a while, in silence, basking in vicarious serenity, and eventually I nod off too. When I wake up, I notice it's just before sunrise. This means I can catch the boats on their way in and get my pick of the catch. I sneak downstairs to slip out the door, not minding that I'm still in the same clothes as yesterday. I race to the harbour to beat the crowds. Just as I'd hoped, there's not a sinner around. I get a good spot at the top of the pier and watch the boats coming in, the birds following them for any loose change they can collect. I think I can see a seal in the distance, but this is most likely my eyes playing tricks on me again.

I pick up what I need and head home, hoping Eve is up and has made breakfast. When I get home I find that Eve and the boys have gone out, but she left some food for me, so I have the place to myself. I don't hang around for too long though as I don't like being here alone; the devil makes work for idle hands and even worse for an idle mind. I'll head into town to see what the goings on are.

Chapter 5 – The veil begins to tear

"Hello doctor, thank you for seeing me on such short notice."

"No problem, I understand the urgencies of your case as well as anyone, I knew you wouldn't call unless it was serious. So how can I help?"

"Mephi's behaviour lately is reverting to what it was like last time just before he was committed to your hospital. He's disappearing for hours on end, coming home with ragged clothes covered in stains. He keeps commenting how I'm his wife and the boys are his kids. At first I thought he was just being playful, but he's said it so many times now I think he believes it to be the truth."

"Hmmmmm, yes. This is worrisome. Is he still taking his medications?"

"I'm afraid to ask him, I don't know how he'll react. But he used to take it every morning with his tea at breakfast, but a few weeks ago he declared he was no longer a tea drinker, and I haven't seen him take the pills since. I didn't think anything of it at the time other than how odd a declaration it was, but now it's obvious to me why."

"How is he with the children?"

"Ok, I think. He's been insisting on telling them bedtime stories which is also a new thing of his. He goes out in the morning; he must be going to the cliffs and the beach because he comes home covered in sand. But he brings a notebook and writes down his thoughts. Then he reads from them to the boys. I told the boys if they act interested, I'll get them a surprise, but I don't know how long we can keep this up. I think he needs to be taken out of my care before something happens".

"Stories? What kind of stories?"

"Just the grandiose, self-indulgent ramblings of a madman. I swear, by the time he shares them he has convinced himself they are real and presents them as so!"

"I see. Thank you for raising it with me, it seems he is losing touch with reality again. I will have a team over by the end of today to escort him back to the

hospital. I assume he'll get aggressive again so best if you and the boys find somewhere to stay tonight. Do you have someone you can stay with for a few days?"

"Yes, that should be fine. I have some family nearby, they've been asking me to visit for a while, but I couldn't with Mephi, so now is as good a time as any".

"Very good. I'll be in touch in a few days to give you an update."

"Thank you doctor, but can I also be kept on as his carer for the paperwork? The financial support it provides really does help a lot".

"Of course, of course, to put it grimly, unless you remove yourself you will be in receipt until the day he dies. You're the only person he has left."

"Thank you doctor."

Chapter 6 - Baggage

Mephi was always the dreamer, always daydreaming. As a boy, his teachers didn't have enough answers to match the unending questions he seemed to have. Questions about things that children usually don't think about; "Since it takes seven minutes for the sun's light to travel to earth and so we see the sun from seven minutes ago, doesn't that mean it could blow up and we wouldn't know for seven minutes? Maybe it already has and we're about to find out..." was one in particular that sufficiently scared his teacher to recommend to Mephi's parents that he should see the school's therapist. The teachers believed these borderline nihilistic thoughts were evidence that he was a high risk to self-harm or to harm other students.

It was just the overactive imagination of a child who seemed to find it difficult to decipher between fiction and reality. In his eyes, if something could be true then we may as well just treat it like it is true. The issue with this of course is when the hypotheticals contradict; a superposition based on probabilities isn't in the realm of the child, so when Mephi asked himself "is my best friend really my best friend, or do they just want something from me so are pretending to be my best friend?" it was a question that perturbed him for months and eventually became such a toxic thought that it infected their friendship until they stopped talking, his best friend never knowing why Mephi became so cold toward him and so held a grudge about this for the rest of their school years together. This, unfortunately, was evidence to Mephi that he was right, and his friend wasn't his friend, he was just being used, although for what exactly Mephi never cared to ask, the betrayal itself hurt enough.

This modality of thinking pervaded Mephi's relationships for the next decade or so, from schoolmates and friends to teenage girlfriends, Mephi couldn't accept that most people were just simple and honest in their actions. They didn't always have a dastardly ulterior motive. Those who grew to know Mephi blamed this lack of trust on the fact he was raised by just his grandmother and was a lonely child. His mother died shortly after she gave birth to Mephi. Nobody noticed the signs, but she was struggling with post-partem depression which was incorrectly self-diagnosed as falling into schizophrenia, as her father suffered with schizophrenia and was constantly cycling in and out of depressive states. She despised having to witness his demise out of sanity and wished he, in her words, "had the decency to kill himself and spare his family the burden of him". One evening, she took a stroll with baby Mephi by the canal, parked his buggy on the bank, kissed his forehead and then stepped into the oncoming gushing waters. She was found a couple hours later downstream, caught up in the weeds, by a family throwing seeds and breadcrumbs to the local ducks. She didn't leave a note or any hint that this was planned, which always haunted Mephi as he grew older. What exactly was the thought that convinced her to leave her infant and end her life. If, in that moment, someone was there to talk to her, would he have grown up with a mother?

The grief of her passing hit Mephi's father hard. He already had a history of psychotic breaks himself too and was overwhelmed by the thought of raising a baby by himself. A few days after his beloved wife's demise, he hung himself from a tree along the canal near where her body was found.

As a result, Mephi's only living relative, his maternal grandmother, took him in. Though she was a person of enormous competence and highly respected in the community, she was old and so lacked the spriteliness a young boy requires from a parent. As such the families nearby to her home were always eager to help with Mephi wherever they could. One week, the Gray's would take him on their family hike. The next, the Byrne's would bring him over for dinner. The eldest brother of the Keane family, Mossy, was a soccer coach and although the age group he coached was a few years above Mephi, he would bring Mephi along with him. Mephi took great pride in laying out the cones for practice and chasing the stray balls that got kicked out of sight. Mossy would encourage him by telling him he was the fastest ball-getter they ever had (technically true, as he was the only one). This sense of achievement and paternal praise was something Mephi craved. The other players on the team who had younger brothers and sympathy for Mephi would bring in the discarded items of their siblings for Mephi to take home, under the guise of "it doesn't fit me so you should take it" to hide their acts of charity so that Mephi wouldn't feel inferior, although he was entirely unawares of his life of poverty, as his grandmother provided all he reasonably needed and he wasn't a child that required much.

As he got older and into his later teen years, he grew into himself. His flights of fancy seemed to die down, or he just stopped sharing them with others. This is when he met Eve, the "love of his life". One could say Mephi lived a double life when it came to Eve. The hopeless romantic, and the really hopeless spacenaut with his own realities to live in. He tried to ground himself as much as he could when it came to Eve, living in her reality was the easiest thing he could conceive of and Eve acknowledged and appreciated his level of agreeableness with her, which contradicted his natural obtuseness with everybody else. He would follow her around the town like a new-born calf following it's mother. He anticipated her needs and desires; a cup of tea before she'd ask, an invite to dinner before she got restless.

These few years were the happiest Mephi could recall across his life. The bliss of young love seems all too brief when you have the rest of your life to look back on it. Despite his amorousness for Eve, he knew that their time together had a strict deadline; she was to leave for college, and he was expecting to be drafted into army service. However, for Mephi this ultimately didn't occur due to medical complications caused by a reported training injury, and instead he spent a significant time in hospital. The official reports explained that, after an explosive device was accidentally triggered, shrapnel struck Mephi in the head, knocking him unconscious for an extended period of time. This was enough to discharge Mephi from duty and also set him up with a disability fund and effectively retire him from any future service. The truth, the doctors knew, was that nothing had hit Mephi but instead the stress of the situation caused him to have a panic attack, followed by an epileptic seizure. Although this was the first occurrence, it was such a dramatic shock for Mephi's nervous system that he developed epilepsy and was now deemed high risk for future fits if under high stress. What the doctors who diagnosed him weren't aware of was the history of psychosis and schizophrenia in Mephi's family and, had they known this, they may have considered alternative treatments other than a recommendation to avoid stressful situations. Mephi came to realize that he was unable to process loud noises and that when exposed to them, would trigger a dissociative state where he would essentially slip into a daydream-like state which, if left unchecked, would result in a reoccurrence of an epileptic seizure. He spent a couple years in the hospital, as they require a two-year run of zero incidences before they can release a patient back into society. Mephi was eventually able to achieve this thanks to the peaceful nature of the facility along with heavy doses of mood stabilizing and sedative medications.

As a result of this divergence of lifepaths, Mephi and Eve also diverged over the years, although Mephi always harboured the notion that they would eventually return to their blissful state.

Eve was more pragmatic about their lifepaths and moved on, dating throughout her college years as one is expected to and eventually marrying a man she met in her first year of gainful employment out of college (or at least that was the official narrative). Whether deliberate or not, this man was the total opposite to Mephi. Grounded, practical, literal, and worked every hour permitted to him. If you left him in a forest and handed him an axe he wouldn't rest until every tree was chopped into firewood. Eve believed this kind of man was the optimal partner to start a family with. Someone who could provide alongside her and to be a good role model for the children, of which they would come to have two, both boys. Eve loved them both dearly, but secretly pined for a daughter; "hopefully the next one" she thought to herself each time it was brought up.

Eve was named by her father after he had a dream that his daughter being born would cause the sun to set one final time before rising up to its highest point and staying there for the rest of eternity, the eve of eternal sunshine. Unfortunately, his premonition and faith-tempting attempt at nominative determinism failed, as chaos and tragedy seemed to follow Eve everywhere she went and to everyone who joined. She lost her father in the war, to friendly fire during a training exercise of all things, depriving her of the honour of her papa at least dying in battle. Her mother lived into old age but not long after Eve's father's funeral, fell down a flight of stairs and suffered a tremendous head injury, leaving her severely debilitated both physically and mentally for the rest of her life. Eve learned quickly and at a young age, life is cruel and the only way to not be reliant on others is to be completely self-reliant. She was a tough kid. She had to be, but this softened when she met Mephi. She was transiently befuddled by his ability to detach from reality and go to places of imagination her hard upbringing couldn't allow her to follow. She never quite developed the ability to daydream, the real world was too harsh and she too vigilant to allow her to escape. So, she stopped trying to understand Mephi and instead just lived vicariously through his fantasies. He often went missing for a day or two and would return with amazing stories. Eve never bothered to ask if these stories were real or imagined as she didn't want to burst the illusion for her or Mephi.

Her bad luck continued with her newly betrothed. As the youngest of the two boys reached school-age, it was discovered he had an aggressive form of lung cancer, which she blamed on the cigar he had every evening after dinner, and he blamed on the emissions of the energy plant not too far from the house. His prognosis was not good, but his rapid descent into ill-health and eventual death was too bitter a pill for Eve to swallow. She had allowed herself to think all of her bad luck was behind her now, for she had a happy family with the perfect children and a loving husband, but now her happiness was evaporating away again, like the last spring oasis in the desert drying up under the hot equatorial sun.

It just so coincided that not long after his passing, Mephi was returning home having finally been released from care. As he had no family, he needed a place to stay, was effectively retired and with him came a carer's pension payment, it made sense for Eve to take him in.

In her diary Eve noted "I met Mephi in school. He was an incorrigible, relentless, kinetic force of boundless creativity. Our classmates marvelled at his ability to come up with new games on the fly and to be referee, score keeper and participator at the same time, while always being fair and never letting the power get to this head. He embodied each role with total commitment, as if he sincerely believed he was each those vocations in the moment. I found that a thrill and loved to be in the outer bounds of his gravity, circling him like a distant exo-planet receiving warmth from a sun but hesitant to get too close lest his solar winds destroy me. He noticed this and seemed to gravitate back toward me almost instantly. We started "dating" but for us, at our young age, that meant merely holding hands walking home from school. I soon found out that what I thought was a sun radiating heat, was a blackhole pulling me in. I crossed the event horizon but somehow, thanks to circumstance and providence I managed to escape before harm had beset me. As I and the rest of our class aged and matured, Mephi seemed to stand still. His body grew, but his mind always seemed to be stuck in the childish realm of limitless imagination. While the rest of us were taking up sports, attending discos and preparing for college and a career, Mephi was obsessed with discovering if Santa Claus was a spy working for the government, or if the eucharist given out at mass was a mind control drug because "there was no other logical reason as to why so many people would go to church every week" (his words). This of course was an endearment when we were young, but that he didn't grow out of it, it became disconcerting."

His modus operandi was that if it can be true, it must be true, and he can be the first and only one to prove it. He always considered himself to be an outlier, the outlier, a genius above the 99th percentile. The universe was nothing more than information and he was the only one able to interpret it, to deconstruct it's patterns and see the truth of reality and it was his duty to harness this understanding and convey it to us mere mortals. I always wondered if he was right, but he became so incoherent it was too dangerous to be around him.

He was committed to the psychiatric hospital at 19 years old with a diagnosis of schizophrenia. After the army, the final straw that lead to his committal, a car engine was revved and backfired, he was convinced it was a panther who roared before being shot by a hunter. He spent hours that day looking for the body, maybe some blood or fur, or even the casing of the bullet. The fact he couldn't find any was only further evidence to him of the grand conspiracy that it was cleaned up and that they were really practicing hunting him. Every unexplained, loud noise was construed as a missed assassination attempt on his life, every stranger was an agent gathering information on him. He began to suspect that his friends were actually body doubles, waiting for the opportunity to eliminate him.

He moved into the hospital full time for a few years, and we lost contact, but I was able to stay up to date on him as, when I went to college, a mutual friend of his Grandmother, Michail, was a lecturer there and was lecturing in a module I was undertaking in my first term. Thankfully it was just for the first term, as we started dating the following summer. He seemed so familiar but also so unique. We dated for the rest of my time in college, secretly of course, as lecturers were not supposed to date students, but we rationalised that away as I was no longer a student specifically of his. After I graduated, I got a job in the college supporting the student services and Michail was promoted to president of the college. As soon I had permanency in the role, and we were secure in the two salaries we bought a house near the campus. It was perfect for starting the family we wanted; a large background surrounded by an old but sturdy boundary wall, trees and bushes running along the end filled with birds and creatures and other life. We installed chicken a coop and adopted as many pets as we could. We ended up with four chickens, two cats and two dogs. We also, pretty quickly, added two boys; Theo and Cal. Theo was our first, and not long after Cal came along too. We were a perfect family or, at least, my perfect family. Then my life fell apart, Michail kept complaining of cuts he had from working in the garden that just wouldn't heal over. Then, chronic fatigue along with a feeling of ache "in my bones". It turned out to be cancer. The following eighteen months he spent "lining up ducks". He created a will, wrote long essays to the children explaining what happened and why. He maximised every waking moment making memories with me. I've never met a better person. To avoid the stigma of suicide, he went on a hunting trip alone and "suffered an accident". Death by misadventure it was labelled. I was the only one why knew the truth. Seppuku is what he called it. He learned of it when travelling in Japan, on tour of a museum. The samurai warriors, when dishonoured, would regain their honour by a ritual suicide that involved slicing into their belly with their short knife, and eviscerating themselves from left to right, causing the guts to spill out. Then, the blade is turned upward to ensure it was a fatal wound. To save the warrior of unnecessary pain, once they had inflicted the damage to themselves and proved their valour, an executioner would decapitate them as an act of mercy, to put them out of their misery. Michail felt he had already been decapitated, at least spiritually. So, the literal was not required for him. His last act of dominating his own fears, proving he was still the master of his own mind.

When he passed away, his death in service, pension and life assurance meant we didn't need to worry financially. Unfortunately, though, he didn't have much family to help with the children, so when Mephi was released (as his symptoms had mostly subsided, thanks to a daily, heavy dose of medication) it made sense and solved a lot of our problems for him to join us.

He was mostly normal, but still had wild exaggerations of importance and conspiracies in the world that involved him, either directly or indirectly. He would wander off each day for a few hours to "walk the dogs" he would call it, which entailed walking aimlessly around the shops to strike up conversations with anyone who would listen to him (this was in his mind, how to participate in the grand schemes of the world and exert influence). While he was out, I would put him to use and task him to run some errands for me.

He had fabricated a tale that he would elaborately enact each evening on his return; he was the doting husband and father and I his loving wife. I can't tell if he believed it or just wanted to believe it, but he played his part with gusto every time. He seemed to ignore the fact that I was a widow. At times it was as if he believed he was Michail, in body, mind and spirit. The idealised, healthier version of what he wished to be. He was nothing close to Michail, but it was easier to allow him to believe in this flight of fancy. His name wasn't even really Mephi, it was Dawn. He read a story once about how the devil's name was Lucifer and Lucifer meant the morning sun. He also believed that Lucifer was actually the hero of the story who

selflessly cast himself as the villain. So he named himself Mephi (short for

Mephistopheles, a synonym for Lucifer) as a tribute, as he thought himself a saviour

in disguise too. He had a way of creating a fiction and then instantly believing in it, of

bending reality, or more precisely, his mind would bend to accept a reality as long as

it didn't break him, as if this "truth" had always existed and was obvious and

inalienable. Although it didn't always work, there were times when he was crystal

clear. Totally aware and self-aware. It always seemed to terrify him to see what he

really was.

Chapter 7 - Daydreams

"Sorry I was late my love; I was awful busy people watching. Eve? .....

Hellllooooo?

No answer. Seems like I've beat them home. I'll get a start on dinner so and

feed the animals. I do love the animals. Cats, dogs, and chickens. They all have a

purpose, like true domesticated animals should. The cat keeps the mice away and I

dare say that my beloved wife loves that cat more than she loves me. I've never liked

cats too much, but I think that's just because they remind me of myself; selfish

vagrants never to be seen until they need something. Maybe that's why she loves me

too.

The small dog is annoyingly yappy but a great intruder-detector, it would bark

at a soft breeze. Not that we ever have intruders, but it keeps her mind at ease when

I'm not home.

The big dog, well, he looks fierce and scary but in truth he would sooner roll

over at the feet of an intruder in expectation of a belly rub, than move to attack. Alas, prevention is better than the cure however and if he looks menacing enough to make any potential intruder move on to the next abode, I'll happily take that as a result. He's also very well-conditioned to being around people. We often mistake conditioning for intelligence, but I suppose they're both functional in their own right.

The best part about training animals is you can train a human the same way. If you're clever, you can do both at the same time without the human realizing it - reward the behaviour you want to be repeated, punish the behaviour you don't want repeated. Simple conditioning. Intelligence however is the ability to observe, assimilate and repeat in a functional output that solves a problem. The problem itself is transitory, but we are interested in the general ability to solve all problems. The issue in discerning the intelligent from the interloper is that while it can be difficult to intelligently create a solution, it is easy to imitate somebody else's solution and save the calories. For example, the first time you hear a riddle, you may not get the correct answer, but if you were to hear that riddle again or any of the variations, you will know how to solve it as you've heard it before and can imitate the answer. That's why most just imitate, they lack the capacity to absorb and create in a novel way. But I suppose if imitation is sufficient then why waste the resources on extra steps. We're back to heliotropism and photosynthesis again. Is it better to be the plant that devours sunlight or the herbivore that eats the plant. Speaking of the sun, I wonder how we will adapt and evolve over time to the different levels of sunshine on the new planets. Well they aren't new planets of course, just new planets for us to call home. We've adapted to the sun as we see it from this planet, our lives revolve around the typical circadian clock. The time of day affects your mood, and the seasons affect your orders. In the mornings your shadow tells a story and in the evening, it listens to it. We'll need to tell new stories soon. I wonder would I be a different person if I were born and raised on a different planet? In what ways would I be similar to this version of me and are those similarities the real, true me because they are consistent no matter how my environment changes?

Anyway, enough daydreaming. This food won't cook itself. Although with nobody else here is it worth cooking? Maybe I'll just jot some notes down in my diary. A few clever snippets for my next story.

What did we say about chess? A king is just a pawn with ego, supported by fools. The queen is the power.

Pocket elves. Tiny creatures that have a magic touch that's lighter than a feather. So, light in fact, that our skin can't feel it when it touches off it. This is how they've gone unnoticed for so long. But I've noticed them, they trust me, and they speak to me when I'm alone. They used to live in trees, but we cut down so many trees they had to move. They moved to all sorts of places. They lived in bird nests but that was too noisy. They lived in rabbit holes, but that was too dirty, and the rabbits kept eating all their food. So, they tried to live with us. At first, they tried to live in our chimneys. It was warm and they had access to the outside or the inside as they pleased, but the soot was too much for them and it caused them to cough. They also lived in the legs of old furniture. They enjoyed it here as the wood reminded them of their natural homes in the tress, but eventually we stopped using wood and moved to metals and composites. They now exist in any free space they can find in any moment, in the quantum spaces that exist when we aren't looking at it. When you do look, they're gone.

I've noticed though that the cats seem able to sense their presence and the elves aren't too fond of that, but the elves use their curiosity against them. Just

as the cats get close, they release a brilliant flash of ultraviolet light that stuns the cats but is invisible to the humans. That's the cuteness of the elves and why they've managed to stay nothing more than fantasy; whatever you expect to see when you see is what you see.

All the elves are interested in is wood, so each night they saw off and extract by the millimetre, layers from table legs as these are the easiest to access, hence the moniker "Desk" elves. Of course, this name is not one that transcends the ages, it is a very modern name as a result of a very modern conundrum, that I created. The proliferation of self-assembled Swedish furniture has meant these resourceful critters must come indoors while we sleep and take back their raw materials to create something with. For their sustenance is creation – with each new manifestation of an idea they are renewed and reinvigorated to repeat the process. They may be immortal but only while they are functional. Like a shark, they need to keep swimming forward.

I also think they steal my socks. I have so many missing single socks. It must be them.

Ok, that's enough for now. Maybe I'll have some tea while waiting for the rest to come home. I haven't had a cup in a while. I'll pop on the kettle and have a read of the paper while I wait, let my mind wander while it boils.

Chapter 8 - Haroon

I get tired of waiting and decide to head to the cliffs for some fresh air. I grab my coat and start walking. My mind is racing about these new events. It turns out a conglomeration of the super-nations had already been to Mars and back. They had set up a colony there and began terraforming in anticipation of the mass migration. The current recruitment that was being pushed as a "first step", but the powers-that-be never let the truth get in the way of a good story. Their hope is that people willingly join because this place has become so uninhabitable it is now a favourable choice to leave this once lush planet for the coldness of space, the treachery and the unknown. It's almost as if they deliberately destroyed here to force the choice on us.

I presented a paper once that suggested when we completed the process of automating all the mundane tasks in society, we could slash the population down to about 500 million, effectively eradicating the working class and replacing it with automation, because nobody wants to clean toilets, giving us the ability to live sustainably with the planet at this population level. This was met with outrage, as if those in attendance believed I was going to start murdering the working class myself to bring the population down. In truth, I think I just revealed their plans to them, and they were unhappy about it, so they tried to discredit me and then later take the credit for themselves.

For those willing to leave and go off-world, "work" was promised but this wasn't true work, it was indentured servitude, which is only one step away from slavery. If you present a person with two options, both terrible (but the one you want them to choose is slightly less terrible), then yes, they choose the less terrible option but to call that a choice at all is to spit in the face of reason. Indentured servitude wasn't a real choice, it was just presented as one to make it easier to swallow for those accepting it.

The original intention was to house this workforce here and connect them via headsets that would enable them to control the android alter-ego worker from afar. The "pilot" would plug in to their headset and this would provide bi-directional feedback stimuli (for example, if the android stepped on a rock that might destabilize it, the pilot will feel this through haptic feedback on their own foot) and supress all other stimuli into the body, such as hunger or thirst, with an intravenous drip feeding liquids and nutrients and a catheters and colostomy bags to deal with waste. The pilot would, for all intents and purposes, be the android and in full control of its movements as if the was their own body. The android would be fitted with sensory receptors to relay in real time to the pilot what is going on so they can react and, for example, move away from a heat signal that may damage the android. From an experiential perspective, the iterations showed that pilots reacted faster and more diligently when those sensory inputs were linked to their own senses, rather than just a display monitor they would see. This resulted in a neural cap with electrodes added to the headset, creating a fully immersive experience for the pilot. One thing they were unable to crack though was the time lag in signal response. Communications can only move so fast, and the distance just couldn't be overcome, so now they plan to ship these pilots off world, to space stations orbiting the planets they are working and/or to small townships that have been isolated and terraformed on the planets and moons. Another issue they're struggling with is the motion aftereffect, better known as the waterfall effect - for the observed phenomena where if a person stares at a waterfall for several minutes and then looks away, they may perceive objects they move their gaze to will also be moving upwards. The motion aftereffect is thought to occur because the visual system becomes adapted to the motion of the waterfall and takes some time to readjust to the absence of motion. This now occurs to those who plug out of their androids after extensive use. They find it difficult to live in their own body after extended periods inside the headset. This is becoming more and more prevalent for the youth too, who are the least in tune with their body as it is. We are already a complex algorithm, with later outputs heavily influenced by early inputs, the embodiments of chaos. We don't know how this will affect the young generation in fifty years. The more data you have about a system, the more predictable it will be so you can control the outcomes. Unfortunately, we're living the inverse. With less data, the more it appears to be random luck. You're a weather system hoping for sunshine. I firmly believe they are filling these good young men with lies to get them on the ship.

Then again, that's how the world has always worked. The ruling class needs a working class to eat. An empire is built on the bones of its followers. The ultimate promise of all of this spacefaring is to create a Dyson sphere around the sun that would power the inhabitants of all the planets and moons that we could conquer. Practically unlimited energy for all would make everyone equal, which is why I don't believe it will happen, or if it did, they wouldn't make it known. The elites have too much to lose by equalizing everything through providing free unlimited energy for everyone. A revolt! Off with their heads! Or maybe they will leave us once it's done and be gone for good, hopefully. Leave the planet to those who stay behind. Those willing to take care of it.

Anyway. I don't know why this bothers me so. It's all unsubstantiated so far, but it seems so obvious to me. But then again, I've always had trouble discerning the obvious from reality. As my reality is different from everyone else's. I feel I have lived a thousand lives, that I am living a thousand lives and each life is fighting to be the one who exists in this world. My mind is not my own sometimes. I find it hard to separate my dreams from my waking my moments. My imagination often feels more real than you or I. What am I to believe, if I can't trust my own senses to tell me what real is.

I sometimes imagine myself as a Prince one on of these new planets and how I would rule, in a future life of mine; Beware flattery! It's a trinket that captures every man's heart and he consumes it until he is poisoned blind. My father, the king told me this before he announced I would be his successor to the fiefdom.

"Everything is going as planned sire."

"Everything? That's suspiciously easy. What are you not telling me?"

"Oh, nothing that can't be handled at the appropriate level. We have a 70% success rate for landing the shuttles, we're only experiencing 40% death before return and the infrastructure build is coming along nicely. We firmly believe we'll be harvesting our first crop of superficial organically grown food by next season."

"Superficially organic crop. When did it stop being so simple?"

"Shall I leave the report on your desk?"

"Yes yes, please. That'll be all."

The hardest part of getting the crops to work is the lack of pollinators. The bees, the butterflies, the bats. So crucial. Even just the common fly has its virtues and value. A fly is an unsophisticated creature with a sophisticated escape system. It uses its eyes to calculate the trajectory of a predator, so to calculate its own escape. The faster you move, the earlier it flees. So, the secret to catching a fly is to move in slowly so it will adjust it's getaway speed to match the slow movement. Then, at the last moment, increase your speed and strike swiftly. This is the key to winning battles. Let them believe you are weak when you are strong. Encourage them to strike so you can defeat them absolutely and swiftly.

The sun is rising. Our fake sun that is, I haven't seen the real sun in so long. This sun mimics it so well, the warmth on the skin, the penetrating adjustment to the eyes. The release of different scents and pheromones through the air ducts to enhance the scene you are experiencing. Today it's the smell of cut grass, a thick green dewy smell that sticks to your nostrils. It makes me think what else we could release through the air ducts to control the population how we want. Antibiotics, vaccines, castrations. Control. The issue with control is, while most who don't have it will play along as long as they have enough to get by, there is a minority who want control for themselves which leads to a revolt. So the key to controlling a population is to weed out who these potential revolutionaries will be and convincing them it will be in their interest to join you, or, where that fails, execution. Not just for them but also their parents, children, extended family. Anyone who may be a sympathiser or who may seek revenge in the future. The more I learn about our race the more it disgusts me. The maladies we carry and hide from ourselves. A broken system stuck in a loop, repeating the same mistakes over and over. I have three options. Seclusion, suicide or mass homicide. I choose seclusion, because it means I always have the other two in reserve if I need them. It repulses me. It sits like hot bile in the back of my throat. But still, I go on. I have to be an optimist. If I wasn't one, id have killed myself a long time ago.

Everyone accepts the idea that all of the individual continents were once one giant: Pangea. We accept that the shift of the tectonic plates pulled the landmasses apart and leaves them situated where they are now – but we never draw out the logical conclusion that those plates are still moving and we will, once again, be one giant landmass when enough time has passed. This is an eventuality and if something is an eventuality, and time is just a flat construct for how we observe the universe (that is to say, as the state of universe moves from one of its current order, to another order, if we select any slice of time we are just selecting the order of the universe as it was in that moment), then that means it has already happened. If it has already happened, then all I can do is be ready for when I am also in that moment that it is occurring. We exist in full knowledge that we will die, but we pretend we don't. We know the universe will end when all of the energy is converted to heat, yet we continue to make frivolous plans day by day. Is it meaningful to create momentary instances of order because it is ephemeral and temporal? I refuse to accept we are destined to end no matter what. There must be a purpose why we are here, why we continue to iterate ourselves through time, to some end. That is my Pascal's wager. I bet my life on it.

I tried to clone myself once but realised it wouldn't work out. Not because I couldn't do it, but because my clone and I wouldn't be able to get along. We would divide the labours of my life until we reached a point that we'd decide to create a third clone who we could team up on and force them to do the painful tasks. This would cause a revolt and the third clone would create two more to overthrow the first two. A battle of my inner personalities? A battle of the classes?

I arrive at the bar and immediately I'm pulled into a conversation in the smoking area:

"What's your issue with them leaving anyway? Let them go I say."

"I'd be happy to let them go, if they weren't intent on taking every resource with them and leaving behind only scorched and salted land."

"Things change all the time. You can't stop change, so embrace it."

"I refuse to accept negative change. Change can be for the good. It doesn't need to be in the image of one man who decides everything for people he has never

met, never will meet. We aren't just coal to be shoved into the engine of his ambitions."

"So, what's the plan?"

"We can bomb all of the ships docked at the harbour before they set off. They have gathered them all for the mass exodus they're planning. If we can pull this off, it'll disrupt their plans for years and they'll have to stop sending lambs to slaughter!"

"How do you plan to do all of that?"

"I know some people. The right people. I have an inside man working at the harbour. I know an ex-army guy who can provide the explosives. I have a cabin in the woods waiting for us to hide out, I've already stocked it with supplies as we speak."

"You seem to have thought a lot about this already?"

"It'll work, trust me."

"Trust. I hate when someone asks me to trust them. The implication being that I lack trust, rather than the more accurate, they are doing something untrustworthy."

"This is too risky for me guys; I think I'm out."

"Coward!"

"Now now, glass houses and stones!"

"Go on home to your wife and play it safe like you always do."

"That is exactly what I'm going to do, and when it blows up in your face, you'll hear me chuckling from behind a nice brew."

At that I storm off. Livid that they tried to include me. Now I've been burdened with the knowledge of their plot! An accomplice that makes me. That wretch. Always has an idea, never a good one! I don't know why I continue to go there. Well, I do. Spite, mostly

I head toward my beach and sit near the two gravestones. I take out my pen and pad in the hope of thinking of a new bedtime story for the boys.

"Did I ever tell you about the magical stone I once found? Whoever held the stone was granted superpowers! Super strength, speed, intelligence, all kinds of powers! But only those gifts the holder already had, for it only accentuated your own natural capabilities up to a super level. But there was a hidden curse on these powers. A cost, that everyone who held it had to pay. For there's no such thing as a free lunch and the more you used the powers of the stone, the more it stole away your vitality, your life essence. For each year you used the stone, you lost ten from your life! And I held it for far too long, even after realising the truth. But I'm still here! Unlike most who come to know how the stone feels in the hand. They rarely died from their advancing old age. No no, because the stone works for whomever is holding it, others who wanted the power were always willing to murder to get it. So it came to pass that almost all previous holders were murdered.

Another power of the stone was that it also granted all of the knowledge that the previous holders had and so every owner experienced every previous owner's death as their own memory. For most, the initial crush of painful memories was too much and they either went insane or killed themselves, often both. For those who could withstand the slings and arrows of this gush of pain, they then set out to achieve great things, either in the name of good, or more usually for their own gain. Despite the tragic ending of all their predecessors, each one after the other believed that their reign would be different, that they would be too clever, too swift of mind and body to ever be murdered. But of course, none of them were correct.

The stone itself was busy gathering life essence from all its users, storing all of their memories that they gained while in its possession. What those using and those who seek to use the stone didn't realise was that this stone wasn't a lifeless, inanimate object that granted powers, it was alive. It had a consciousness. And it also had the ability to identify and lure in the weak minded to commit murder and steal it, so that it could continue to parasitically live off a new host. It also had an end goal, once it had absorbed enough life force, it could burst forward, a big bang, and take a new form, filled with life and vigour.

What was the new form? It was a dragon – the ultimate legendary beast! It wasn't a stone at all, it was an egg. The true apex predator and hunter of man. For dragons are the worst fears of man. They breathe fire, fly fast and silent, claws and teeth bigger than the biggest Tiger's you've ever seen, used to crush bone and flay skin. Their body is like a snake, scale and shiny. Their fangs filled with venom.

What was the dragon called? He became known as Haroon the Pestilent. He was jet black from head to toe, with red eyes. His scales were shaped in such a way so they didn't reflect light. He slept during the day and hunted at night, so the only time you were aware of him was through the shadows from his own fire just before he torched your body to ash.

The real reason Dragons horde gold is because they know how foolish we are and that we will risk our lives to get it. So instead of hunting out the nearby tribes, Haroon made an agreement with a village next to the mountain he chose as his home. They would mine all the gold out of the mountain they could and bring to him 90% of it, the remaining 10% they could use for trade. There was a caveat though, as Haroon knew word would spread of this village filled with gold, and greedy men would come calling. If anyone asked where they got the gold, they were to tell them from the cave on top of the mountain, that there was an old dragon there who slept on a bed of it and if they were clever enough, they could sneak in and take some and the dragon wouldn't stir or notice. For this deal, Haroon agreed to not eat any of the villagers or their flock, as he knew that more than enough gluttonous men would walk right into his abode, and he could feast on them. As dark and calculated as this was, Haroon also had a sense of humour. He would play tricks on some of the thieves, so to better understand them and for those he liked, he would let them live and take the gold they sought. Which only added to the myth of the friendly dragon with gold to spare and encouraged more to try their luck. Do you remember what that's called? When you base your decisions on only those who come back?

Survivorship bias. The story only worked because people could only hear it from the survivors. Imagine what they would think if they could hear from the dead! All dead due to their greed and the hunger for power that brought the egg to life. The worst intentions of men create the dragons that come back to haunt them!

To add to the legend of Haroon, the villagers created a children's song that would spread far and wide, so all knew of the dark dread:

Oh grimly, ghastly death did come,

With his scythe and bony thumb,

He danced and twirled and gave a cackle,

A fearsome sight of deadly hackles.

He spoke in tongues and ghoulish tones,

Of ancient realms and buried bones,

Of souls set free and endless sleep,

And graves where mournful widows weep.

With death you bring a final peace,

A timeless rest, a sweet release,

Though we may fear your hollow grasp,

We know you come to end our task.

So when your time has come to pass,

And death approaches strong and fast,

Remember that it's not the end,

It's just the start, my old friend.

As the dragon got older, he realised he didn't really need to eat so much anymore. But he still didn't want to be bothered by thieves and he didn't want the word getting out that he was no longer a ferocious flesh-eater, as this would mean he would turn from predator to prey. Though he maintained the relationship with the local villagers, instead of eating those who attempted to visit and thieve, he bartered with them instead.

Leave your animals for me to eat and I will allow you to flee, on the condition you tell your people how ferocious I am and how I should not be trifled with, there is not enough gold in the world to be worth it!

And so, they did. The myths and the stories spread far and wide of the most ferocious dragon that ever lived. Atop the highest mountain that only a fool or hero with no regrets could even attempt to climb.

Of the animals, it grew to be fond of them and found uses for their natural proclivities. The goats tended to the grass outside, the pocket elves kept the inside tidy and inventoried. Yes, even the Pocket elves found a home here.

One day, a group of soldiers from a faraway kingdom marched to the foot of the dragon's mountain and declared this mountain to be theirs and that the dragon must leave immediately. The dragon knew this to be an empty threat, as there was no way they could harm him. So, he ignored them. In reply, the army deployed a trick the dragon didn't think of. The sounded all the trumpets they had at once, as loudly as they could. The sound rang and echoed throughout the valleys of the mountains until a giant avalanche started. The dragon felt the ground shake and flew up into the sky to avoid it. After it settled, he flew back to his lair to find all of the animals he cared for now crushed to death under the avalanche..

He was so enraged he flew to the base of the mountain and killed every soldier except for one. He allowed one to live so he could return to his kingdom and tell everyone how ferocious Haroon the Pestilent really was. After the last solider left, Haroon called upon the leader of the local village to request a favour of him:

"The animals. They were my friends. Please, bury their bodies with dignity and as payment you can have all the gold in my mountain. No harm will come to any from your village who cross my threshold. You have proven yourself the only ones worthy of my trust."

The village leader replied "You humble me, great dragon. We will of course carry out your wish, but no payment will be required."

"It is not a payment. A bounty earned is not payment but a debt to be cleared. I will have no debts, especially not to a noble people. As to what I will do next. I will clear one other debt I owe, to whichever king sent that army that defiled my mountain. He will learn my I am called the Pestilence."

"I see. May I request something of you, great dragon? Please, wait three days before you seek this king. Allow me to send a messenger to the peasantry of his lands, to seek refuge from the fire that you will reign upon them. For these are innocent. This will also give time for us to prepare the funeral arrangements of your friends. You can observe it and then set off, having seen your kin onto the next life."

"Very well, use the riches you have earned to care for your people and whatever people you can attract from the kingdom. In three days, whomever have chosen to stay have chosen death."

The hours passed and on the third day, a great ceremony was held and the funeral pyres were lit by the dragon himself. As the smoke blocked out the moon and the only light visible was from the base of the fires, Haroon took flight into the sky with a great thrust of his wings which cleared the smoke in one sharp whirlwind and left the gathered villagers in awe of the dragon's might as he flew away like a bolt of lightning. The village leader had successfully exfiltrated those from the kingdom who weren't involved in the warrior king's escapades. They snuck them out in the dark of the night on the third day, purposely waiting until the last moment to avoid suspicion or detection.

At night, the streets of the kingdom are normally bustling with life and energy of the locals, drinking and trading. This night, it was still, quiet. You could hear the moon whispering, the trees breathing in followed by a long exhale, they knew what was coming.

And that is the story of the dragon. A story that has no end, as nobody knows how it ended. Haroon was never to be seen again and this time, the dragon left no survivors.

Chapter 9 – The Garden

I keep getting this feeling I did something terrible. Like an old memory, or a lucid dream. It feels like it's true, but I can't quite tell if it is. It creeps up on me, always about to reveal itself, only to then fade away. What scares me most is I can't say I wouldn't do it, whatever it is. For I have no bounds. I know I'm a terrible person. I feel like I've been dead for years and I'm just been waiting for it to catch up with me. This isn't about you! You self-righteous sanctimonious prick. The world doesn't unfold through yours lens of perception. It affects everyone and so do your actions. If you want to destroy yourself at least have the fucking courtesy to not destroy everyone else with you. Why does my mind treat me so. I've lived like a shameless man and so I should die like a shameless man. I deserve to be stuck on this forsaken rock.

"Tend to the part of the garden you can reach."

"I'm not sure you could call this pile of red dust a garden."

"A garden is whatever your mind makes it to be."

"My mind makes it a red pile of ash."

"You trust your senses too much youngling. Your senses are just a translator for you to understand a language you don't speak, but you are trusting that the translation is honest and true. It isn't, it is abbreviated, contextualised, and bastardised in a way that a simple mind, your simple mind to be precise, can process. The higher mind has to see what isn't visible, to smell what isn't odouress, to touch the ether and recognise the noxiousness of true reality and not just the pleasantries and lies our senses present to us."

"Am I to take that as an insult?"

"You can take it whatever way you wish. Now, please tend to the part of the garden you can reach first.

"Why can't I come over and help you."

"Hubris. How can you help someone else if you haven't done it for yourself yet. Prove your ability to help others by first helping yourself. Be an example for them to follow."

"Or I could just be a nice person and lend a hand where I can."

"Everything in time. For now, we just need disperse the seeds everywhere and see where we get lucky."

"Can do!"

Short and sweet, like a ripe pear. I do miss the taste of pears. The environment here is too harsh for most fruits to grow and the canned foods ran out long ago, or so they told us. I do suspect they have some in reserve, either for a special occasion or for a special guest, but I have searched through every nook and fossek of this place to no avail. Damned pears.

We arrived here at some time in the last decade, how long exactly escapes me. Also, my brain is too connected to the circadian day cycle back home, I can no longer track time here with any accuracy. Our job was to terraform and colonise it by any means necessary. They wanted to create a second home here, or a new first home. The real home they created was the behemoth spaceships they sent us here in. If we had the fuel to sustain us, I would argue our future could be on those ships, living in the gravity of a nearby resource rich planet or moon like the nomadic hunter gatherer we once were, but alas we haven't gotten that far yet, or regressed to it, I'm not sure. Each ship had a farm with livestock and vegetation, imitation beaches for exercise with faux sunrise and sunsets, they even periodically created misted mornings which smelled and like salted seawater. Subtle control by duping the senses. We had schools and restaurants, sports courts, dog areas. It also had lots of pregnant women which delighted those onboard to see the next generation of life to come along with us, but the cynic in me believes this was to expedite the adaptation period, to acclimatise faster and see how the body would adapt to developing in the differing environments and gravity. All passengers were volunteered and had all expenses covered, plus a dowry paid to the family upon leaving just to sweeten the deal, which really meant it was targeted at the poorer, working-class families. They were told it was to be a round trip, but then, while on the journey outbound, it was announced that a nuclear war had started back home making it impossible to return anytime soon. I believe this is a convenient lie to keep the workforce they've invested so much into, although I keep this conspiracy to myself, I don't want to make unnecessary enemies. I also keep it to myself as I am aware of the deleterious effects an idea can have. The wrong idea can be a parasite. "People don't have ideas, ideas have people"! Ideas are a skilled parasite that moves from person to person until they find someone who can achieve and fulfil the idea. It is a formless, shapeless thing that fits to the mind of the person thinking about it. They don't go out of existence, just out of body for a time, or into hibernation. Waiting for the moment the individual is weak enough to be conquered. Sometimes they kill the person hosting it. Sometimes I think ideas are generated by the universe just to create some chaos.

"The garden is finished, twelfthed with all seeds dispersed and watered."

"Twelfthed?"

"Yeah, you said divided it into twelve. So halved is divided into two, quartered into four, twelfthed into twelve."

"Hmmm, sound logic but I don't think that's the correct term."

"Why do you judge people based on how they speak?"

"Because your words are how you choose to represent your mind and I know how excellent your mind is, so I want you to harness it and show it. Some, and by some I mean most, unfortunate people can only speak in a cultural shorthand because they don't have the capacity to self-generate thought and speech. You must understand that your intelligence is directly linked to and driven by the body. If you can run fast, it's because you have legs that are capable of it. The bones, the muscles, the connective tissue. To be intelligent you have to be capable of being intelligent, and part of that is the ability to tolerate insults, both physically and mentally. If your nervous system is not durable, you can't tolerate the slings and arrows to be intelligent. If you can withstand more assaults on your nervous system, it enables you to process information through a greater amount of intellectual filters. The imbecile can't handle the attacks on the mind and so never goes beyond the first layer of thought, and this is reflected in their speech. So you need to rise above the expedient

urge to speak lazily and instead use your brain to communicate the precise message you wish to convey so that you aren't misinterpreted. For good communication is in the language of the listener."

"I never thought of it like that. I suppose you're right."

"You suppose?"

"You are right. Thanks grandad. You're the only one who talks to me like I'm also an adult instead of a child."

"You're definitely not a child, you're an adult in training. It's my duty to train you with whatever knowledge I can pass on before I go."

"Go where?"

"Nowhere in particular, I just won't always be here."

"Do you want to go home?"

"That's a good question. I certainly would like to go back to the Talam of my youth. Peaceful, plentiful. I think for now we're better here though. At least based off what they tell us about home. Our best bet is to stay here and make it work. Besides, we don't have the option to get home, no ships have returned in a long time. We're here for good."

"I know, I just wish I could see it once."

"I'm sure you will, eventually. Suns almost setting, I promised your mum I'd have you home at a reasonable time so you should get going. I'll be here again tomorrow if you'd like to help again. "

"Thanks Grandad, I will. I'll come by for an hour after school."

"I look forward to it!"

I find it difficult to cry. I know that's a learned deficiency and I should be able to, but it's been so long that crying in the presence of someone feels like an act of self-indulgence. I'll tend to my own wounds after everyone else has been tended to. If it can be endured, endure it. Don't make a show of courage, or cowardice.

"What are you writing on today?"

"Oh just some thoughts I've been having lately. You can read it later after I've digested it and don't feel shame about it anymore."

"Wonderful, I look forward to it!"

I like to write in the morning before the rest of the world wakes up and before my ideas are spoiled and tainted by the insidiousness of the presence of others. I've always kept a journal in some form, since I was a young man. A prisoner I guarded in a previous life mentioned he was keeping one mentally, to tell the story of his people when he eventually got free. I thought it was cute he believed he would see freedom. I knew the die was cast, and that I would be executing him in the coming days.

Writing is all I really have as catharsis these days. We've been off world and on this planet for so long I find it hard to believe we're still even the same creatures. I have no concept of time anymore as it feels we are constantly under the sun and the parts of our brain that had any autonomy are overridden by the augmentations. I suppose I'm fortunate enough to have the augmentations, though they charged me, literally but no pun intended, an arm and a leg for them. For the workers, they're now closer to apes than the civilization we left. Working them so hard, treating them so poorly, leaving them to govern themselves in a constantly starved state has left them like wild animals. Like a domesticated pig returned to the wild, it will become a boar again not too long after, developing a more muscular build, growing longer tusks, and becoming more aggressive. Beastly.

The previous owner of this plantation was a gentle fool who despised the idea of slavery, serfdom or servitude. However, that wasn't apparent to the external observer. From the outside, it looked like any other slave house. The wealthy inside, the workers outside. This old man might have been a fool for sentiment, but he was cunning in his actions. He made an agreement with each slave he bought – "come work for me and you will be treated like an equal, with fair reward and conditions and for every profit we turn together, I will free another slave just as I've freed you. You will be free to leave my house at any time you wish, but I promise, the conditions will be more hospitable to you than you will find anywhere else on this planet for your kind". How could they say no?

It came to be that his slave house became the largest and most profitable house on the continental shelf, yet nobody outside the house knew its secret. This operation continued for almost forty years before the old man eventually died. At this, the owner of the second largest house(that would be me, good reader) saw an opportunity and made an offer to the two sons of the deceased to buy their fathers house for a very generous sum. The sons were torn, for this was a mighty offer but they also feared their fathers good work would go to waste if a new owner came in. So they politely rejected the offer and set to work to continue where their father left off. As time passed, they realised the operation had become so big and their lands so vast it would be best to split it in two, with each governing their own half. This happened many times over, to where they stopped managing lands directly, but had emissaries running the divided operations for them and reporting upward. This resulted in making the sons eminently replaceable. So I encouraged my most loyal confidantes that I employed to apply for their emissary jobs and kept in close contact with them. Once in situ they nurtured division and insubordination at my request. From the shadows I organised dissent and planted provocateurs. Soon, the brothers were at war with each other, both distrusting the other and blaming other for their trials, for they knew it was someone with intimate knowledge of them causing these problems.

I waited for it to reach a climax and then I reached out to both of them, separately and quietly. I offered assistance, guidance and resources. They both came to trust me, the pseudo-father figure they never really replaced but always yearned for. I encouraged them to broker a peace, to meet on neutral ground, my ranch, with just their trusted emissaries to accompany them. They both agreed and over dinner I murdered them both. The witnesses, who were their emissaries secretly working under my command, all corroborated my story that they murdered each other and the emissaries were handsomely rewarded for their congruity. All's fair in love and war and I considered this war.

I continued their fathers tradition, not because I'm a good man like he was. In fact, I deliberately ruined his reputation by spreading misinformation amongst the workers "What they didn't know was that any slaves who did choose to leave were hunted down and captured in secret, on the dime of the old man. He tortured them under a different name and then let them go, so they would return to his house with tales of how terrible the outside world was, so that the others were too scared to leave!", Hah! Fools. The reason I continued his ways was because the old dullard happened to stumble upon the perfect strategy for domination. Convince the worker that working hard is in their best interest. Share some of the spoils with them as a reward and over time, reap greater and greater self-sustaining profits. I placed my sons as viceroys in my stead, for they already knew the operations and I basked in my unending success.

You might think I'm an evil man, but you must realise there is no such thing as evil. You should abandon your framework of right and wrong. It doesn't exist. There is only the adaptive and maladaptive extended iterative successes and failures. Morals are just a layer of abstraction, a social contract that we apply to reality to help comprehend it as a pseudo-hivemind. This is not a tragedy of the commons, but a tragedy of the common people, and there is nothing common about me. We are a godless animal trying to live by rules we created but with no true inherent reason behind it. If there is no god, then there can be no sin. Without sin there can be no crime. For myself? I rebel against the meaningless of the universe by creating my own pocket of meaning and bliss. Just from spite. I can live in spite. Some people must live for something. Some people must live against something. I live against everything. My heart pulses hatred and beats disdain. I inhale tragedy and exhale travesty. The world can burn for all I care, as long as I get to have my tea.

Like I alluded to, as a younger man I was a prison guard. Well, that was a glorified name we used when someone outside would ask what we did. In reality, we were "confession extractors", i.e., torturers. I have my favourite methods, depending on the person and how you wanted to break them. To psychologically break someone, get them to admit their mistakes in the promise it will bring them salvation. Then reveal it won't and their admission was for nothing. The admission shows them the shame they have been hiding from. Then, solitary isolation. Leave them alone with nothing but water and their regrets. Their mind will waste away faster than their body until they either become homicidal or suicidal. Either is fine with me. Before that though, is the physical torture. A person who is able to have a fingernail removed and not break will be able to have all ten removed without breaking. That isn't to say you shouldn't remove them, you certainly should. For one, it's remarkably gratifying. Secondly, you can't let them think they have won a battle, or you will lose the war. If you stop because you know they won't break, this will encourage. But if you proceed, if you pursue every nail, they will realise the folly of their ability to not break, that it will be in vain as the torture won't stop. They will realise it will be for nothing and they will accept domination. However, we can be tactical. Remove the nails on one hand, then call for a toilet break. Leave the captive alone for some time to think, to contemplate. Then, in the silence, have two guards, down the hallway and just within earshot, mention how another prisoner talked after only five minutes of torture! The coward! The wretch! The traitor! Allow some time for this information to brew in the mind of your stubborn prisoner into rage, into insult. Then, give me that other hand so we can remove those other nails. Now, NOW, dear reader, the unfortunate soul will think "I have conquered my torturers and survived, I have kept my secrets and suffered, but why must I be the only one? Why should I continue to suffer when they have already learned what I know, but from another." A reasonable conclusion and before you pop another nail off, he will relent. Reluctant acquiescence. The mark of a vanquished foe.

This however does not always work. Sometimes they don't overhear the conversation, too much blood ringing in the ears. Sometimes they've gone into shock to deal with the pain. Sometimes their mind abandons them, and they go insane. Not to worry, we always have enough bodies in the cell that we can find enough people who will break. Then, at the end of a shift I leave the camp and I notice the beauty of a sun that has fully risen. It takes me a few moments to adjust to its light. As I hold my hand up to protect my eyes I wonder, does the suns warmth feel as pleasant on everything it falls on? I suppose only if you're in a position to accept it as warmth. The fools in the camp cells are experiencing the same sun I am, but they aren't enjoying it like I am. The privileged and depraved drink from the same well but it quenches them differently.

As a youth, the quality I valued most in another was intelligence and how they could use that intelligence to challenge me. A young man is concerned only with destruction because you can't contribute to a world that's already perfect. I now see the folly of intelligence. How it misleads. Half of the men in the prison are smarter than I, but here I am, on the outside enjoying my freedom. The highest quality is integrity. If you can't tell the truth to yourself, how can you tell it to me. If you can tell the truth to yourself, then everything else becomes circumstantial. What is truth? If you are dead and I living, you can't object to what I claim to be truth. I will stay true to myself by lying to everyone else. One stranger is no different to another stranger, so a group of strangers is just one. A collection of individuals is just a larger representation of one. That's why most people aren't really themselves. They're an output of their zeitgeist, an amalgam of the cultural shorthands they've absorbed in the attempt to relinquish responsibility of autonomy, so that their failures could always be externalised. Cowards. Any semblance of bravery from them is always an unintended consequence of some other cowardly action. A single butterfly in a room won't land on you, but a million butterflies in a room will eventually lead to some landing on you out of nothing more than chance. Outsourcing your moral compass in this way makes you a slave to the tides of change. This is why I have hatred and disdain for everyone. I don't take solace in pretending I believe in God or culture. I despise sympathy. I'd rather live with a concealed wound than advertise it to lower expectations of me. I wish the sun would explode and kill us all. Maybe it already has, and we won't know for another seven minutes. We're already dead. Omae wa mou shindeiru. I don't seek forgiveness or apologise for myself; to do so would be to commute my sentence onto those I've transgressed against, doubling the insult to them. So, I hold their malice, like Atlas holding the world.

Chapter 10 - Medb

"Never odd or even. Undecidedly rigid. For this briefety I'm in possession of a soul. My soul. Only it's not mine forever. I must choose how to use it before it slips away. Fragile yet steadfast. The ether awaits. Generativeness precedes it."

"Medb, what are you up to?"

"Oh, I didn't hear you come in."

"Is that why you were startled? What are you up to?"

"None of your business. I was writing some poetry."

"Can I read it?"

"No, you can't."

"Why not?"

"Because it's not finished yet."

"What's it about?"

"I don't know yet really. I'm still figuring that out."

"Well, what's it kinda about?"

"I think it's about my fear of death and how I feel the need to create something meaningful before I die. How constant creation and renewal is the only thing stopping the universe from ending. How everything is always in absolute chaos but also in perfect harmonic balance."

"Wow, ok. Grim. Sorry I asked."

"Life is grim, so we should treat it grimly."

"The protest march is about to pass by, thought you might want a look at it."

"Yes! Thank you! Let's go."

After a brave whistle-blower revealed that the Government had in fact already sent a number of ships off-planet over the last two decades, a series of other whistle-blowers from different nations followed suit and this caused a revolt around the world. Not because the Government were doing things outside of public knowledge, but that they had lied to them about being the first to go now. This, as you can imagine, created a lot of conspiracies as to why they hadn't told us of the previous missions. The main consternation was the conspiracy that all the previous expeditioners were either dead or left off planet to die, and the next batch would meet the same fate. The unfortunate reality of the matter is that this was indeed the truth. The previous missions had been a total failure and they had run out of bodies to throw at the problem. All missions either ended with explosions and death of ships and crews, or mutiny caused by distrust and sometimes insanity. Or, simply, ships that went beyond the ability to communicate with and so they were left to fend for themselves, with no knowledge of what has happened to them since. Little did we know, some had made it successfully and were continuing with the mission, assuming the cavalry would arrive any minute. Good Romans indeed.

Outside of the conspirators and protestors were a significant number of people who were willing to believe the prevailing narrative. Previous missions were test only and with small numbers, the majority of whom returned safely. This encouraged plenty of those in need of work to continue to apply for the jobs as they believed it was still their best opportunity to provide for their family. So they threw themselves into the cosmic winds, at somebody else's problem in the hope their sacrifice would mean a better life for those they loved, consoling themselves with the belief that they were more valuable dead than alive.

The protests continued down the streets and Medb, the diminutive firebrand teenager who disagreed with everything, joined as it passed her home, jumping straight into the middle.

"NO MORE GREEN LIGHTS, NO MORE RED LIGHTS!" The protesters sang as they went. Medb shouted it too, but she didn't know what it meant.

"What are the green and red lights?" She yelled to the person next to her, trying to get above the decibels of the singing crowd.

The stranger replied *"They don't tell the volunteers where they are going, so the only way they find out is based on the lights at the front of the ships when they are taking off, green light for Planet A and red light for Planet B. We don't even know which is which yet, we only know this much because one of the ships malfunctioned at the last minute before take-off and they had to evacuate. Some were injured in the evacuation and were moved to the hospital and were able to tell the details to their loved ones, although once the decision makers found out this was happening, they swiftly moved them into an army hospital with no visitors allowed. They're basically enticing the lower social classes in the door with the promise of well-paid indentured servitude and then turning them into slaves as soon as they get them in."*

"That's horrific! How are they getting away with this!"

"It's too hard to stop them because we don't know who they are. The government says it's a quango but we think that's just so they have plausible deniability for all of this."

"What's a quango?"

A loud, sudden bang and crack penetrated the air and stopped the chanting and marching in place. Around the bend a large police force had gathered, and they were in full riot gear, ready to charge them down. Before the protestors knew it, they were being hit with a barrage of water cannons and smoke grenades. They immediately dispersed in a panic down nearby side-streets and into any building that didn't have a locked door or window. Anyone unfortunate enough to be left in the street once the smoke cleared was arrested for what they called rioting and looting. This included Medb, who was trampled over by the escapees, as she was not expecting it but it seems like those around her might have been.

"What's your name little one?" Asked the constable back at the station.

"Do I have to answer that?"

"You don't have to do anything, but it would make your life a lot easier if you did."

The not-so-veiled threat worked, as Medb's calm demeanour was no match for the imposing situation she found herself in. Still, she was clever enough to figure a way out.

"I'll write it down for you, nobody gets the spelling right."

"And how do I pronounce that?"

"Like the Month of May, with a soft V at the end."

"Thank you Medb. Now, how did you end up here?"

"You arrested me".

"Clever. And right before I arrested you, why were you there?"

"I didn't mean to be, I live a just few minutes away, I was leaving my home as the march was going by and I tried to cut through it, but they caught me up into it. Thankfully you broke it up or who knows where I would have ended up!"

"Well, I suppose you're welcome then. Run along home and be careful about getting involved in any future protests, you'll only get the benefit of the doubt once!"

"Thank you, good sir, I promise I won't."

Lying came easy to Medb, she could usually figure out what the other person wanted to hear and then use that to get what she wanted. She bolted back home, excited about her taste of adventure and her brush with the authority. In her mind she bested them and this was thrilling. This would be enough to satiate her rebellious tendencies for a while.

Chapter 11 – Death and Rebirth

Upon arriving at the cliffs, Mephi sat before the two gravestones and started to cry. After a couple of minutes, he heard the ruffling of feet behind him. It's dark now, but he can make out the flicker of torches. At least six of them. Finally, a face is recognisable, the doctor. Upon seeing that old face, Mephi wept *"I killed them, I killed them!"*.

This causes a panic, and the doctor immediately signals to one of his accompanying staff to contact the police to ensure Eve and the boys were ok.

"I killed them! They didn't deserve it. They were too young and innocent, but I couldn't stand that they had two parents that loved them and provided for them! Why were my parents taken away! Why did nobody care for me! I killed them and buried them here, under these graves and placed the headstones myself!

The doctor and his team had been inching closer to Mephi as he ranted and were in place to sedate him. They restrained and medicated him and carried him back down the hill and into their transporter. Upon arriving at the Psychiatric Hospital, he was committed, and placed into his old room. After a while, Mephi woke up in a place he found all too familiar. The sterile aesthetic was too pure and clean. He immediately asked for a cigarette.

"I haven't seen you smoking in a long time. You haven't been yourself at all lately".

"Really? I smoke all the time. You must not have noticed. I feel like I'm more myself today than I have been in a long time".

"It sounds like you're about to reveal a grand deception."

"That's the thing about deception, it's all smokes and mirrors…"

The nurse doesn't appreciate my attempt at humour. A man will laugh at your joke before the punchline, to performatively show how clever he is that he figured it out. A woman who figures it out early will instead wait until the end out of politeness. This is why women are superior to men and why men fail to see it. Why do we laugh anyway. Is it evolutions way of advertising intelligence and humility? Who knows. Maybe a cigarette is just a cigarette. I do find it is a great way to breach a divide. If you don't have anything in common with someone, you are required to build from zero. Humour is usually a good place to start. Although most people won't even make that little bit of effort. They require a pre-existing shorthand and a belief that the commonalities are inherent and meaningful, rather than just circumstantial and ephemeral. I find the fewer things in common the less meaningful the mediating factor needs to be. For example, in my travels abroad I've often found that just sharing a language with someone is enough, even if you have different nationalities, and even if those nationalities would otherwise be at odds with each other, strength in numbers and two is greater than one. I've always found speech and language to be amazing, particularly in how they create themselves. We tend to think we created language, but it creates itself, we're just the vessel for it. Given that our languages are older than any living person, how they morph from regions and dialect. The English of Shakespeare might as well be a different language to English of today, yet we believe them to be one and the same. How could we create that? Millions of people acting in unison without explicitly agreeing the rules of engagement? Nonsense. English and all languages are a self-creating virus that have enslaved us. But, like a sophisticated virus should do, it doesn't kill the host but instead empowers it to thrive. Eventually, one language will prove superior to others, and we will all speak it. It's been well documented that to truly commit a genocide of a people you extinguish their language. Kill the virus at its source. Force them to speak your language so the virus will transform them to be like you.

"The doctor is here to speak to you and provide your medications."

"Medications. Why do you insist on this sadistic torture. You push me to the brink of death and then stop, allowing me to recover only to start afresh. I don't want anything from you, just to be left alone, to not feel the pain. Let me die with some honour.

"We can, but before I have a few questions. Last night, you claimed you murdered two boys and buried them on the cliffs. Who were those boys you mentioned?

A long silence held over the room before Mephi responded.

"In literature and society, it is always commented that a mother's love is unconditional, absolute and to be revered. I contend it is to be reviled. It is self-serving, for the mother is endogenously rewarded with a pleasureful chemical cascade each time she engages. They are gluttonous monsters who devour their children for their own appeasement, to ease their anxiousness. All love is selfish, a person only comes to love another when they realise they will receive more in return than the price they have to pay to receive it. You aren't in love with the other, you are in love with self-preservation. I have never been in love, I just liked the idea of someone loving me, for if they saw the true me how could they not fall in love?"

"You've claimed many times that you were in love with Eve? Was this not the truth?"

"That was not me. Not the me that stands here. That was another version of me. One capable of it."

"I see. Will that version of you be joining us at any time?"

"I don't think so, he and the others have gone into a slumber."

"When the others are you, are you not there anymore?"

"No, I'm always here. I just feel different in the moment."

"I understand. We should discuss that more later but it is important to stay on track right now. The gravestones you mentioned?"

"I don't remember. It was so long ago."

"We had it excavated and there was nothing there. The stones that you called headstones, that you claimed to place there. We checked those out too and they were just commemorative statues placed by the villagers for an anniversary. It wasn't a grave at all."

"I see. Doctor, can you tell me, what is real."

"Well, that is a question. Can you be more specific?"

"Medb, the old man, Eve?"

"Well, Eve is certainly real. Who is Medb?

"She is me, in another life. I can live many lives in many bodies across time and place. I understand the true nature of time and the universe."

"Oh? Are you doing it right now, or do you mean reincarnation?"

"I don't know. These feel like my memories. I am these people. Or am I?"

"It depends on what you mean when you say "I". To you, can you tell me, what does "I" mean."

"I don't know what I am. I am Eve's husband."

"No, Eve was married to someone else, he died a few years ago. Do you remember? Then, when we stabilised your condition, we were able to release you back to your family but, Eve was the closest thing to family you had. Eve tells me that you quickly tried to fill the shoes of her late husband, acting as if you were her husband and father of the children. Yet you never shared her bed. You always slept on

the sofa downstairs. Tell me, why would a husband not share a bed with his wife? Deep down, you know this is a fabrication, don't you?"

"That's the problem. It isn't that I can't tell what reality is; I can't tell what the fabrications are. You hear a car engine; I hear a lion roar. You see a murder of crows; I see the shadow of a dragon. How can you expect me to live in a reality I don't exist in or perceive. "

"I don't expect anything of you. I'm just here to listen and to try to help."

"I think it's clear I can't be helped. Just leave me in the padded cell, I can entertain myself."

"We can arrange that if you'd like."

"I would. Please. How is Eve? She won't talk to me about anything."

"She's good. I think she's relieved you're gone, as you were starting to become unreliable, but she's sad you couldn't maintain your health. The boys keep asking for you too, they miss your stories."

"Do they? Good. Can I have pen and paper in my cell, I can write some new stories for them as my mind wanders."

"Of course."

"One last thing, doc?"

"Sure, what is it?"

"Are we really on another world? Or did I imagine that too?"

"Oh, no, you didn't imagine that."